loving the BILLIONAIRE HEIR DOC

dobi daniels

Luxhaven
Publishing

ISBN paperback, 978-1-958987-00-1

Interior Design by Luxhaven Publishing

Cover Design by The Book Brander Boutique

Editing by JD Book Services

Proofreading by Lisa Lee Proofreading

To JC, Grandma D, and DC, whom I love more than life itself.

Dexington Doctor Billionaires Series

Loving The Billionaire Heir Doc

Loving The Billionaire Owner Doc

Loving The Billionaire Army Doc

Loving The Billionaire Cowboy Doc

Loving The Billionaire Boss Doc

Dexington Christmas Billionaires Series

A Billionaire Inventor for Christmas

A Billionaire Butler for Christmas

A Billionaire Dentist for Christmas

A Cowboy Loves the Doctor Series

A Doctor Second Chance for the Rancher (prequel)

A Doctor Blind Date for the Cowboy

A Doctor Enemy for the Cowboy

A Doctor Billionaire for the Cowboy

Standalone

Her Billionaire Nemesis (short story)

Thank you for choosing LOVING THE BILLIONAIRE HEIR DOC. I loved writing the story of Alicia Montgomery and Blake Dexington. Their love story was the first one that came to mind when I started thinking about the Dexington Doctor Billionaires series.

It's so easy to stop loving yourself or to believe no one can love you when you make mistakes that change the course of your life. I pray LOVING THE BILLIONAIRE HEIR DOC gives you the hope to believe that love is still possible no matter your past.

Please continue this journey with me in

LOVING THE BILLIONAIRE OWNER DOC, which is the story about Josh, Blake's best friend. You can grab your copy at https://dobidaniels.com.

Would you like to be notified when the next Dobi Daniels book releases? Sign up at https://dobidaniels.com.

Once again, thank you so much for purchasing LOVING THE BILLIONAIRE HEIR DOC and for meeting Alicia Montgomery and Blake Dexington. If you enjoyed it, please consider leaving a review at your favorite retailer or recommending it to a friend.

Thanks again for your support!

Dobi Daniels

Loving the BILLIONAIRE HEIR DOC

Alicia Montgomery's heart raced and threatened to escape from her chest. It was a familiar feeling, one that happened whenever she stepped into this place.

Not that this room was any different from the other offices in this section of the hospital, with a small examination bed backed into the left corner and its light blue walls filled with painted sketches of cartoon characters. But this was the only place that made her feel small, afraid, and unsure of herself, which was strange given how intimate she was with the hospital.

Alicia was a second-year internal medicine resident at Dexington Medical Center and walked the hospital corridors daily to attend to patients. But it was like that familiarity didn't matter in this one room—here, everything was personal, and she was just a concerned caregiver.

She was grateful that Dr. King had been able to squeeze her in this early to accommodate her busy schedule. She'd started a new rotation this morning and had already been at the medical wards since six-thirty a.m. to see her patients and complete a pre-round with her team—two interns and a medical student. She had then attended the morning report where another resident had presented a patient's case for discussion.

But Alicia hadn't been able to concentrate, and her mind had drifted to the upcoming clinic appointment with Dr. King. She'd snuck out as soon as the discussion came to an end and had arrived at Dr. King's office a few minutes later. She only had about twenty minutes before she had to rush back to join the attending round.

Serious dark grey eyes stared back at her from an unusually sharp-featured face with a prominent aquiline nose. A red bow tie peeked out from beneath the white coat that Dr. King wore as he sat opposite her, a dark brown desk between them. But the tie was askew, and Alicia was tempted to straighten it—anything to help keep her mind from what the doctor had to say.

Instead, Alicia focused on the tall mahogany bookcases bulging with medical books and journals that stood as sentries on either side of the only window in the room. But she didn't really see the books per se—they just allowed her to look everywhere but at him.

She let out a sigh, and the sound filled the room that had been silent save the quiet hum of the HVAC system in the background and the occasional distant cry of a child from the hallway. She couldn't keep running away. It was time to face the music.

Dr. King rested his elbows on the desk and leaned forward in his chair. "I have both good news and bad news," he said.

Alicia didn't want bad news. She'd even worn her lucky outfit—a grey straight skirt with a light blue button-down shirt—under her medical coat, for good measure. But it was time to get it over with. She drew a deep inhale and smoothed back an errant lock of long dark hair away from her face. The sooner she heard what the doctor had to say, the faster she could leave this room.

"Let's start with the good news," she said, her voice coming out with a squeak. Her face tightened at the sound. *Get it together, Alicia,* she thought. *You can do this.* She cleared her throat and sat up straighter as she ran her hand down the front of her white medical coat.

"Can I get you some water?" Dr. King asked softly.

Alicia shook her head. She didn't trust herself to speak.

"Okay." He stared at her for a moment as if deciding the best way to continue. "Let's start with the good news. There is a new treatment protocol that may be helpful for Willow. We've been researching it for some time, and early results have been promising."

Alicia's face brightened, and her gut unclenched. Willow—her niece—hadn't taken well to the current treatment protocols that seemed to work for other children with cystic fibrosis and had spent most days in her short life in the hospital. So any treatment that gave her a chance at living a somewhat normal life was always welcomed.

Dr. King leaned back in his chair as he continued speaking. "However, as you know, there are always risks involved, even some we may not have identified at this time. But we still believe Willow is a good candidate for this protocol."

Alicia stayed silent. She was no stranger to treatment or procedure risks—she told patients about them every day. No doctor worth his salt could say otherwise. But that didn't stop Alicia from worrying about how the treatment protocol would affect Willow.

She crossed and uncrossed her long lean legs. "What kind of risks are we talking about?" she asked.

"The treatment might trigger acute episodic coughing and shortness of breath for many days to weeks. In a worst-case scenario, it could cause pneumothorax or respiratory failure. But we'll be monitoring her closely to handle it if and when it occurs."

Alicia didn't doubt they would. Willow had a great team here at Dexington Medical Center —they had saved her life multiple times. The hospital had the best cystic fibrosis program in the country, and it was the reason Alicia had transferred Willow here. Alicia had become Willow's guardian after Willow's parents— Alicia's only sister and brother-in-law—died in an accident. But having the best team didn't completely put Alicia at ease. It wasn't the same when it concerned someone close to her.

She winced as pain shot through her hands. Alicia looked down and realized she'd gripped the chair's arm tightly. She released her hands and rubbed them together before letting them fall on her lap. She still needed to hear every-thing before she could relax. "What about the bad news?" she asked, her tone belying how she felt.

Dr. King's face remained expressionless as he spoke. "Unfortunately, our research grant is unable to cover all the treatment costs. We expect the patient's family to cover the balance either out-of-pocket or through insurance."

Alicia shifted in her chair. A heavy feeling settled in her stomach. Money issues had of recent become a sore point with her. "How much are we talking about?" she asked.

"About fifteen thousand dollars."

She squeezed her eyes shut and could feel a full-blown headache coming on. Fifteen thousand dollars. This was worse than she'd imagined. She couldn't afford it. Medical residents weren't paid a lot, and most of her salary went to paying off Willow's medical bills and the interest on her student loan. There was no way she could squeeze out fifteen thousand dollars.

It was at times like this that Alicia wished she had someone on her side. Someone to share the burden with even if it was just to talk through options. But that was a pipe dream and not reality. The truth about her would be too much for any sane man to bear. And she couldn't afford to get hurt again. She could do this alone—she had to.

"We would also need to start the treatment protocol in two weeks," the doctor continued.

Alicia's eyes jerked open. "Two weeks?" she blurted out.

"Yes, two weeks. As you are probably aware, Willow hasn't been doing too well on her medications lately. We don't want to think about what would happen if she continues this way."

Alicia's chest tightened. Willow had seemed weaker this week, but she had chalked it up to a slight change in her treatment. Maybe she had refused to acknowledge what was right before her eyes—Willow was deteriorating.

Alicia choked back a cry. She couldn't afford to lose Willow—not now, not ever.

Dr. King leaned forward. "Dr. Montgomery, we believe that if we start this treatment soon, it might improve Willow's chances. The earlier she gets enrolled, the better her prognosis will be. She could have a good quality of life where she could actually live at home, go to school, and play like any other normal eight-year-old," he finished with a reassuring smile.

Alicia stared at the doctor's face. He seemed very confident about the treatment. Maybe Willow had a real chance this time around. There was no choice when it came to matters concerning Willow—Alicia would do everything short of selling herself to make sure Willow got better. Which meant she had to ensure that Willow was enrolled in this treatment program. She had to get the money no matter what, even if she couldn't see how that was possible.

"Okay, I want her in the program," Alicia confirmed.

"Good." Dr. King typed a note into the computer. "Why don't you speak with Carla in the Billing Office to figure out if there are any financial options that could help?" He stood up and walked around to her side. His portly figure gave him a fatherly look that was otherwise hidden when seated.

Alicia got up as well and grabbed her leather tote from the seat beside her. She looked at the clock on the wall behind his head and noticed that her appointment time was up.

Dr. King led the way to the door. "I've already given Carla a heads-up, and she should be expecting you," he said. "Why don't you call me as soon as you know what the final arrangements are?"

Alicia flashed a weak smile and nodded.

Dr. King smiled in return as he pulled open the door for her. Alicia held herself ramrod straight as she stepped out of the office and eased the door shut behind her. The hallway was empty—there were no other patients waiting outside his office.

She let out a heavy sigh and leaned against the door for a moment. Where would she get the money? She took a deep breath and let it out.

The best thing right now was to see Carla.

Hopefully, Carla had good news, or else Alicia wasn't sure what she was going to do.

Alicia looked around the office while she waited for Carla to finish what she was reading on a computer that sat facing her on her small brown desk. The cream-walled room seemed tiny, with its mini-cubicle-like dimensions that could only accommodate the desk and two compact chairs for visitors.

The room seemed a tight fit especially for Carla, a jolly, buxom five-foot woman with short brown hair who seemed to enjoy eating her donuts as much as she loved giving them out. The rest of her work surface was piled high with disorganized documents, a myriad of pens, and sticky notes visible between the papers. The smell of freshly baked donuts resting on a mini tray—where it seemed at home perched on a small corner of the desk—tickled Alicia's nose, and her stomach growled.

Alicia grimaced. She'd had no time to grab breakfast before heading to the wards. She darted a glance at Carla, but it appeared she hadn't heard the noise.

Carla clicked out of whatever page she had been looking at and anchored her attention on Alicia. "I've checked with the insurance company, and unfortunately, Willow's insurance does not cover experimental treatment."

Alicia struggled to steady herself, hope seeping from her like air from a deflated balloon. Even though there was no guarantee, she had expected some portion of the costs to be covered. Well, it had been worth a check. She tucked a piece of her hair behind her ear as her mind struggled to think of other alternatives she could explore. But it seemed that particular well was dry.

However, it appeared Carla hadn't finished. By now, beads of sweat were sprouting on her forehead, despite the cool atmosphere. Alicia watched as they coalesced to form rivulets that ran down the side of her face and then her neck. Carla pulled a white handkerchief from her black jacket and dabbed them away. "So, I looked within the hospital to see if there were any funds or grants that Willow might be eligible for. Fortunately, she qualifies for a five-thousand-dollar grant from the Elaine Hartford Memorial Fund, which supports caregivers in covering medical costs for children with genetic diseases. I put in an application yesterday and got a confirmation this morning that Willow has been approved for it."

It was like a boulder rolled off Alicia's chest, and tears welled up behind her eyelids. If only she could reach over and plaster kisses on Carla's chubby cheeks. But Carla would think she was nuts. She smiled instead and leaned back on the metal chair. "That's good news," she said. For some reason, the chair was not as uncomfortable as before.

But Carla rubbed her fingers on her furrowed forehead. "That leaves ten thousand dollars that you still need to cover."

Alicia nodded. Funny, she wasn't as worried as before. *The five-thousand-dollar grant must have done a number on me*, she thought. Like it had pierced the veil of worry and brought Alicia back to her senses.

Alicia couldn't think of any sources at the moment to raise the money, but she knew they had to exist. *I'm not going to give up*, she thought. Willow would get the treatment no matter what it took. Alicia straightened up in the chair and held Carla's gaze. "Thanks for checking, Carla. The five thousand dollars really helps. Don't worry, I'll figure out a way to raise the remaining money."

Carla responded with a tentative smile. *Seems she doesn't really believe me*, Alicia thought. Well, she was going to make it happen. She watched Carla make a few notes on the computer.

Alicia's phone buzzed in her coat pocket. She pulled out her phone and looked at the screen. *Shoot*. It was the alarm, reminding her about her next appointment. If she didn't hurry, she was going to be late for the attending round, her first in this new rotation, which wouldn't speak well of her. She stood up. "Thanks, Carla." She didn't wait for a response and hurried to the door.

"Good luck, and let me know how it goes," Carla's muffled voice echoed from behind her. It sounded like Carla was back on the donuts.

Alicia stepped out into the hallway and closed the door behind her. Her mind swirled in a whirlwind as she hurried down the hallway. Ten thousand dollars. It didn't seem as daunting as fifteen thousand dollars had. Was she now seeing the glass as half-full instead of half-empty? No matter. The most important task now was to find the money even if she had no idea how—to fill up the glass so to speak. *Help me, God,* she prayed.

She would find a way to make it work for Willow no matter what it took.

Because she had to make up for all the wrong she'd done.

There was no other option.

*B*lake turned on his side and opened his eyes. He could see rain cascading down the glass that encased his apartment, giving off a dream-like effect. He'd missed this view. It was one of the reasons why he'd snapped up this apartment a few years ago, the other being that it was located in one of the most sought-after areas around the hospital.

The seven-thousand-square-foot penthouse suite boasted floor-to-ceiling windows that provided a two-hundred-and-seventy-degree view of the city's skyline, and featured three bedrooms, an office, a gym room, a full kitchen and dining area, a large living room with a state-of-the-art sound system, and custom Italian furniture. It opened up through double doors to a wraparound terrace.

Blake placed his hands behind his head and stared up at the ceiling. He'd just dreamed about a dark-haired beauty that had fascinated and enchanted him. It had been a long time since a girl had piqued his interest, in dream or reality. But even if it was a sign, he was ignoring it. No one else had held his interest after Miranda, and not for lack of willing girls who loved the idea of who he was. And even that relationship had been a disaster. A nightmare that he didn't want to revisit. What was it they said about being once bitten, twice shy? That was him. So, relationships were a no-no as far as he was concerned.

Blake shook his head. This wasn't the time to be thinking about love, especially after arriving early this morning from Boston. He had been completing his internal medicine residency at one of Boston's top hospitals, but a call from his father had changed everything, and Blake had agreed to return. His father had pulled the strings to have Blake transferred back to Dexington Medical Center to complete his residency. It would have been impossible otherwise, given that the second year of residency had already started.

And it wasn't a step down in any way—Dexington Medical Center ranked consistently in the top five teaching hospitals across the country. He had begged off work for a few hours this morning with the plan to join the attending round. Even though he hadn't officially connected with his team, Blake had gone straight to the hospital once he had arrived, to see the admitted patients that would be his going forward.

Blake stretched out his arms wide and yawned. It had been a grueling night before coming to Dexington—he had come off a night float. He didn't need to look in the mirror to know that his eyes were bloodshot—it would go away once he was out and about. Blake was no stranger to hard work and impossible schedules. He had juggled medical training and business school at the same time, graduating with both an MD and an MBA in four years. And it didn't help that his family was part of society's elite. Blake was expected to be exceptional, and he hadn't disappointed.

Blake turned his neck and looked at the

alarm clock on the nightstand. His eyes widened. He jumped out of bed and raced to the bathroom in his boxers, his feet silent on the heated floors that ran throughout the penthouse. Today was the first day of his General Medicine rotation, and Blake could not afford to be late for the attending round. He'd been informed that the departmental chair was going to be there— she was a stickler for punctuality. Getting on her bad side on the first day was not an option. Thank goodness his apartment was close to the hospital. If not, there was no way he could make the round on time.

He took a quick shower and headed into his walk-in closet to get dressed. Fifteen minutes later, and dressed in tan slacks with a light blue button-down shirt and brown loafers, Blake opened the coat closet by the door and grabbed his white medical coat. Based on the weather forecast, he could still make do without a fall jacket. His medical coat would be enough.

Blake's stomach growled, but he ignored it. There was no time for breakfast today. He could refuel at his favorite hole-in-the-wall joint a few blocks from the hospital after the ward round.

Blake walked through the foyer and entered

his private elevator. His phone pinged in his pocket. He pulled it out to see a text message from his father—Blake now had an appointment with the departmental chair right after the round. This was yet another reason why he couldn't afford to be late.

He rode the elevator down to the underground parking lot where his red convertible was parked. He would have preferred to walk since the hospital was only five blocks away, but he could save time if he took the car. Besides, it was raining cats and dogs, so it made more sense to drive to the hospital.

Blake jumped into his car.

He could still make the round on time if he hurried.

CHAPTER 3

Alicia looked at her watch as she stood at the entrance of the administrative building, where the billing office was housed. She now had only a few minutes if she wanted to make it to the attending round. This was one round she couldn't afford to miss—her department chair was going to attend, and Alicia was a big fan of hers. Dr. Hartwood was very successful and seemed to have everything together, just like Alicia wanted for herself.

Alicia pulled an umbrella from her tote and strode down the side of the driveway. The torrential rain pelted down on her umbrella, leaving everywhere wet and murky. Alicia pulled her coat tighter around her body and quickened her pace.

As she hastened through the rain, her mind continued to search for options to raise the money for Willow's treatment. The last payout from her sister's accident had all gone to clear Willow's latest medical bills. Her current pay as a resident was a pittance compared to all the bills she had to pay, including the interest on her student loans. She'd already emptied the nest egg she'd saved from her part-time gigs in college and medical school in getting Willow transferred from Boston, where they'd lived with her sister and where Alicia had gone to medical school.

She'd been lucky to get part-time research work that meshed well with her very busy residency schedule. It only worked because Alicia was used to operating on very little sleep. Still, the money from it wouldn't be enough. Maybe she could stop paying the student loan interest for now. But it wouldn't make a dent in what she needed. *Lord, I really need a miracle*, she prayed.

No matter how much she racked her brain, no other solutions came to mind. She sighed and turned right at the end of the driveway and headed toward the main hospital building. She was familiar with this route, so it was easy to avoid the puddles of water on the sidewalk.

Gripping her umbrella over her head with one hand, Alicia looked at her watch. Her heart beat faster. She only had three minutes before the ward round began, and she quickened her pace.

Then she heard a low rumble on her left. She turned her head to see where the sound was coming from, and a red convertible car zoomed past, splashing dirty road water all over her.

Alicia squealed and jumped back further away from the road, but it was too late. She looked at her coat. The damage was already done. Globules of mud and streaks of brown water decorated her formerly pristine coat. As the rain fell all around her and washed debris down the street, Alicia felt it wash away her chance of making the round on time. There was no way she could attend the meeting in the condition she was in.

"Hey!" she shouted at the car, but the car didn't stop.

Alicia's nostrils flared, and her body tensed.

Unbelievable! Whoever the driver was, he should have stopped to apologize. Did he think driving a sports car made him special? This just reinforced her feelings about the so-called privileged.

Well, she was going to get her apology. Looking to see that the car had made a right turn ahead, Alicia guessed the driver was heading to the hospital entrance. She could make it there if she hurried.

It was time to put her college running skills to good use.

CHAPTER 4

*B*lake could barely see the way ahead despite the efficient *whoosh whoosh* from his wiper blades—a never-ending stream of rain from bulging dark clouds beat down hard on the car's windshield. Even though this type of weather in November wasn't new, the intensity of the downpour was unusual. But the climate never seemed to make much sense these days. He'd heard the talking heads say global warming had changed everything.

Blake glanced at his Rolex watch, a birthday gift from his father. Seven minutes left. *I can still make it,* he thought. Up ahead the lights turned yellow then red. Blake grumbled under his breath as he slowed his car to a stop. He tapped his fingers on the steering wheel. *Come on, come on,* he thought. He could see the outline of the hospital jutting out far ahead beyond the trees, which meant the turnoff to the hospital entrance was only a few yards away.

The lights turned green. At that moment, an old man bent at the waist and dragging a shopping cart stepped onto the pedestrian crossing. He was soaking wet despite his rain poncho. Blake resisted the urge to press the horn and waited for the old man to cross fully to the other side. His mother had raised him right.

As soon as the man reached the other side, Blake shot his car ahead. On any other day, he would have slowed down, but he needed to get to the hospital fast.

He checked his watch again. Five minutes left. If he sped up a little, maybe just maybe he might be able to make it on time. He accelerated and headed for the turnoff to the hospital's entrance.

Dexington Medical Center was the main hospital for Dexington Healthcare—a sprawling network of hospitals, health plans, physician organizations, physician specialty groups, and other health-related companies. The seven-story brick and grey stone building stood tall and erect with manicured grounds encircling its back. It was flanked on the right by the hospital's administrative building, and on the left by a connected accident and emergency building extension. Visitors to the hospital could either valet park their cars or park in the large garage building that was across the street but connected to the hospital by a walkway.

Blake decided to valet park today. The parking garage got full pretty quickly in the mornings, and he didn't have time to drive around and search for an empty spot. He arrived at the hospital's main entrance and pulled his car behind another waiting vehicle.

The area was a beehive of activity. The heady smell of pansies, chrysanthemums, and balloon flowers from the back gardens married with the aseptic smell that floated out in the air as patients, their families, and hospital staff streamed in and out through a large central revolving door. Caregivers pushed wheelchair users up the disabled ramp and in through dedicated automatic entrances. Valets darted between cars as they directed vehicle drop off and pick up.

Blake jumped out of his car and drummed his fingers on its roof as he waited for his turn. He craned his neck over the cars to see if there were any available valets, but there were none.

Just then, he heard a shout. He turned his head to see a dark-haired, long-legged beauty hollering like a banshee and headed full speed in his direction. If he wasn't in a hurry, it would have been amusing. As she got closer, Blake could barely make out what she was saying. "Hey, you!" he heard her yell.

Blake looked behind him. There was no one standing there. It seemed he was the target of this human tornado.

The young lady barreled closer with her hair whipped all over her face—he couldn't make out her features. Her stained medical coat failed to hide her lithe, gorgeous figure.

Blake felt a jolt in his system, and his heart raced. She was stunning, even though she seemed mad about something. He sucked in a quick breath. *What's going on?* he thought. It had been a long time since he'd felt this way.

"Here you go," a voice said beside him, bringing him back to reality. A young man in a valet uniform held out a ticket to him. Blake gave him a brief smile and accepted the ticket in exchange for his car keys.

He looked at his watch. One minute left. He wished there was more time; it would have been fascinating to find out what the bombshell wanted with him.

Casting a regretful glance at her, Blake turned and sprinted toward the hospital entrance and through its revolving doors.

"Hey!" Alicia shouted out as her feet crunched to a stop at the beginning of the hospital entrance. It had been a while since she'd run this fast—apparently, she still had the goods.

She saw the driver turn to look at her as he stood beside his car. Other sets of eyes swung her way, but she ignored them. She probably looked a sight—that didn't matter right now. She was only focused on getting the driver to apologize for splashing dirty water on her. The fact that he looked like he'd just stepped out of a magazine with his startling blue eyes did nothing to deter her anger. It seemed to fuel it instead. If he thought that looking like a six-foot

GQ model gave him an excuse not to apologize, he had another think coming.

But Alicia didn't expect what happened next. He suddenly took off in the direction of the hospital's revolving doors. It took a moment for her to realize what was happening. He was actually running away!

Alicia's face tightened. "Oh no, you don't." She pivoted and raced towards the doors after him.

She halted as she entered the hospital lobby and looked right then left. She couldn't find him in the sea of medical staff and patients hurrying to different destinations in front of her, their feet clacking on the smooth tiled floors. A quick look over the expansive area, with its whitewashed walls lined with seats where hospital visitors lounged and a popcorn stand in a discrete corner, yielded nothing. The young man was gone. And asking about him from the folks at the central information desk was out of the question—she didn't even know his name or who he was. Where had he disappeared to?

Her phone alarm beeped. Alicia slapped her forehead. *Ouch.* She'd been so carried away with getting back at the driver that she had forgotten about the round. This was really weird behavior for her. She was now certified late. She felt the headache that had somewhat receded coming back again, and she rubbed her temples. The day couldn't get any worse.

Alicia had to fix the situation. First, she needed a clean medical coat. Good thing she had already put a spare in her assigned locker in the on-call room. It wouldn't do to appear at the round looking like a wet cat, and on her first day nonetheless. Second, she had to clean herself up and get rid of the stains on her clothes as much as she could. It was a good thing that the coat had received most of the splatter. This she could attempt in the restroom. She had no spare outfit in her locker except for scrubs, and donning them would make her stand out more, since it wasn't a practice to wear them for ward rounds. She could always change into clean scrubs once the round was over and before she started attending to her patients. For now, she would just button up the coat as much as she could and hope no one noticed anything.

Making a beeline for the elevators, Alicia hastened to the resident on-call room. She would deal with the errant car driver later.

CHAPTER 6

"So glad you could join us, Dr. Montgomery." Alicia froze. How had the professor known her name? Over sixteen pairs of eyes turned to look at her. *Oops*. What a way to create a great first impression with her favorite professor. It would have been better to just disappear into the ground.

She had ended up seven minutes late and had snuck into the back of the group. No one else—the other attendings, residents, interns, medical students, and even the nurses—had seemed to notice, so Alicia hadn't expected the professor to out her.

She flashed an apologetic smile as heat crept up her face. The professor stood at the head of the group and frowned down at her through her silver-rimmed glasses, her short silver-grey hair framed in a bob around her face. Dr. Hartwood was the chair of the internal medicine department and a professor of gastroenterology. She was also gorgeous, with clear porcelain skin and a body that belied her age. A perfect mix of beauty and brains. Many of the medical students, residents, and attendings aspired to be just like her. It was a privilege to be able to attend one of her ward rounds.

Alicia drew in slow steady breaths. It was all the driver's fault. "Wait 'til I catch you," she mumbled.

"What did you say, Dr. Montgomery?" the professor asked.

"Oh, nothing." Alicia ducked her head while her hand twiddled with one of the earpieces of the stethoscope in her coat pocket.

The professor waved Alicia forward. "Since you are so keen on sharing your thoughts with us, why don't you tell us about the next patient, Dr. Montgomery?"

Alicia craned her neck to see what patient the professor was referring to, and her shoulders relaxed. It was her own patient. Awesome. She had already seen her this morning, so she was familiar with her case. The group parted as she made her way to the front, and then she was standing at the patient's side.

The professor stood next to the head of the bed where the patient, a plump middle-aged woman with brown hair pulled into a chignon, reclined at a forty-five-degree angle. A machine beeped next to where she lay, and a bouquet of flowers was nestled on the nightstand on the other side of the bed. The group was standing in a semi-circle around the foot of the patient's bed, which was located a few steps away from the room's large windows.

Alicia felt all eyes on her. Well, it was time to redeem herself. Good thing she had never had stage fright. She took a deep breath, acknowledged the patient with a nod of the head, and turned towards the professor. "This is Mrs. Carter, a fifty-five-year-old woman who presented at the outpatient clinic with difficulty in swallowing solid foods which had worsened over the course of a year. No history of difficulty in initiating swallowing, pain on swallowing, heartburn, chest pain, or difficulty in swallowing liquids. Only relieved by vomiting—no relief with Zantac or multiple swallows. And no worsening with cold foods. Patient noted that she may have lost some weight; she has not been on any diet."

The professor looked at Mrs. Carter. Alicia could guess what was going through her mind since she'd thought the same thing. Thank goodness Mrs. Carter had noticed the weight loss—it would have been hard to observe otherwise, seeing how great she looked.

Alicia put her hands in her medical coat and continued. "No medical history of allergy, asthma, cardiac disease, fever, rashes, or recent travel. No history of drug abuse, alcohol, or smoking. Mrs. Carter has no pets and is not on any medication.

"Physical examination showed a normal nasopharyngeal cavity, clear lungs, a normal cardiac rhythm with no murmurs, and a normal abdominal exam. No enlarged neck lymph nodes or thyroid masses. No motor or neurological abnormalities. Rectal examination showed a slightly bloody stool. Differential diagnosis included peptic stricture, esophageal carcinoma, motility disorders, and Schatzki's rings.

"Her blood cell counts were within normal

levels from the lab results. Barium swallow revealed a small mucosal lesion with a narrowing of the distal esophagus. No rings or motility issues were found. Endoscopy confirmed a moderate chronic inflammation of the esophageal mucosa and a small mucosal mass. Biopsy of the mass confirmed Stage 1B squamous cell carcinoma of the esophagus. Mrs. Carter has been seen by the surgeons and is scheduled for transfer to the surgical unit."

The professor nodded appreciatively. "Thank you for the nice summary, Dr. Montgomery. Anything else?"

Alicia stayed quiet for a moment. What had she missed? Something niggled at the back of her brain, but she couldn't recall what. "Nothing comes to mind," she said.

"Anyone else have anything to add?" the professor asked the rest of the group.

The group remained silent. *The medical students won't say anything even if they know,* she thought. Only the attendings and residents would respond. No student wanted to be the one that made a resident look bad.

Then Alicia heard a rich, authoritative voice from the back. "Mrs. Carter has recently been prone to spontaneous bouts of tears." The group turned to see who had spoken.

Alicia's stomach clenched, and she kicked herself mentally. How could she have forgotten this observation? The night nurse had mentioned it to her when she visited the patient this morning, and she had even noted it in the progress notes. She blamed the omission on her distracted mind from the incident this morning. *Wait till I find you, you car driver*, she mused.

"Mrs. Carter would wake up and find her pillow soaked with tears," the voice continued. "The nurses noticed the same when changing her sheets. But there was no excessive sweating on her skin, and her room is maintained at a cool temperature."

Alicia couldn't help noticing that the sound of the voice did strange things to her insides. It was melodic, soothing, commanding, alluring, disarming, all rolled into one. Alicia could feel it driving away the tension and beckoning to her at the same time.

She searched around to identify the owner of the voice. Who could it be?

Her eyes alighted on the speaker, and she gasped.

Blake noticed a change in the demeanor of the stunning young female resident who stood next to the professor. How he'd been able to focus on her presentation was a wonder, given that he couldn't take his eyes off her—she was tall, just the way he liked, with long legs that went on for miles and skin that glowed with health.

He'd been held under the spell of her soft brown eyes—framed by long curly lashes that twinkled with passion as she spoke, but which also hinted at a certain vulnerability. She maintained a graceful pose even as her dark upswept hair threatened to cascade around her face. She reminded him vaguely of someone, but he couldn't remember who.

Blake stiffened. It had been a long time since he'd reacted this way to anyone, and it felt unfamiliar. But then he'd sworn off relationships for good reason. And he couldn't afford to get distracted, not now when his father needed him. First, it had been the lady at the hospital entrance and now Dr. Montgomery. Maybe the dream he'd had this morning was making him vulnerable. *Get yourself together, Blake*, he thought. Dr. Montgomery was a colleague and could be nothing more.

"What do you think could be the cause of her tears?" The professor's question broke into his thoughts and drew him back into the present.

Blake blinked. Now this was familiar territory. "Mrs. Carter lost her husband five years ago. They'd been married thirty years, and yesterday was the anniversary of his death. I believe Mrs. Carter may have been mourning the loss of her husband and could benefit from some grief counseling," he concluded. He had noticed her tears when he'd come by to see his patients and had asked the nurse-on-duty about her. He'd planned to bring it up with the resident-in-charge of her case as soon as he could, but then this opportunity had presented itself.

He couldn't help stealing a glance at Dr. Montgomery, and he noticed she sported a frown. *I wonder what's on her mind,* he thought. *Wait, but you are not supposed to be thinking about her.* He pulled at his coat and forced himself to focus back on the professor.

The professor gave him a brief smile and addressed the rest of the group. "It's important to consider every aspect of the patient's life while we treat them. No detail can be considered too small or inconsequential. Unresolved grief in this case could inhibit the effectiveness and outcome of any treatment she receives."

The professor then turned to Mrs. Carter. "I'm so sorry for your loss."

Mrs. Carter nodded in acknowledgement, her head bent as she tried to hold back her tears.

The professor drew the attention of the attending closest to her. "Let's send a consult to Psychiatry for a psych assessment," she said. The attending nodded in reply and whispered to one of the residents to get it done.

The professor turned back to Blake and smiled at him. "Good work, Doctor."

Blake smiled in return. This was the aspect of medicine he loved—being a part of helping a patient recover. He was happy that Mrs. Carter would receive the support she needed.

He felt eyes boring into him and turned to see Dr. Montgomery glaring in his direction.

Blake rubbed his brow. What was her problem? He'd just made sure that her patient got the help she needed. She should be thanking him instead of throwing darts at him. Strangely, he found her reaction intriguing. But he ignored the pull to figure out why—that would be going down a rabbit's hole, one he might not be able to come out of. So Blake turned all his focus on the professor.

The rest of the ward round went off without a hitch. All the newly admitted patients were seen by their bedsides, and updates on the old patients were discussed. Soon, they had adjusted the treatment plan for the last patient. The group moved out into the hallway and began to disperse as teams—an attending, his residents, and interns— broke off either to conduct their team-specific management rounds or to attend to their long to-dos.

Blake saw the professor say something to Dr.

Montgomery and then walk away, but he had no idea what they'd spoken about. He walked over instead to where his team stood, introduced himself, and explained to his attending that he had an appointment with the department chair. The attending gave him leave to go, but asked him to come back and catch up with the interns later, which was fine by Blake.

His phone buzzed as he left the wards. It was time to meet Dr. Hartwood and find out what his father had planned for him—any thoughts of Dr. Montgomery would have to stay behind.

Alicia couldn't believe it was the handsome jerk who had splashed water on her earlier today! Mr. GQ was not only a doctor in this hospital, but a fellow resident in her General Medicine service! She had heard the rumors last week that a new resident was joining them, but she'd considered it impossible since the residency matching exercise had been over a few months back. Even though the Electronic Residency Application Service—ERAS—was primarily for interns, second year residents could still be matched and transferred through the same process, as long as they had the necessary sign-offs from the department chairs of their current and prospective hospitals.

It took only a minute before all the anger she'd felt at him came rushing back. Not only had he made her late, but he'd had the audacity to also make her look like a fool! Especially given he was the reason she'd forgotten about Mrs. Carter's tears in the first place.

Alicia's hands clenched into fists. A tiny voice at the back of her mind told her that he'd actually helped, but she ignored it. Of course, she was happy that the patient was going to get the support she needed, but did he have to be the one to point it out? She probably wouldn't have been upset if it was anyone else. *You are not going to get away from me this time*, she thought. She would confront him at the end of the round.

But as the meeting ended, Alicia found Dr. Hartwood beside her. "Dr Montgomery, I need to see you in my office immediately," she said.

Alicia's eyes widened in surprise. What had she done wrong? Before she could ask Dr. Hartwood, she'd walked away with one of the other attendings.

Alicia looked around to see if she could spot Mr. GQ, but he was nowhere to be seen. Well, it seemed he was good at the disappearing act. But now she knew how to find him.

She still had a long day ahead of her, and now she had to see Dr. Hartwood first. There was no time to waste if she wanted to finish everything she had on her plate.

So Alicia left the wards and headed to the professor's office.

~

Alicia took the elevator to the fifth floor and headed toward Dr. Hartwood's office. The door was slightly ajar, and she stepped in to see the professor's secretary on the phone. The secretary waved at her to go in. Alicia gave her a brief smile and knocked at the inner door before turning the knob to step in.

Dr. Hartwood was standing by the window behind her desk and appeared to be on the phone. She gestured at Alicia to grab one of the seats facing the professor's desk. Alicia noticed that there was someone already occupying the second seat. The person turned to look at her. It was Dr. GQ!

Alicia's fists clenched. She didn't know whether to laugh or cry. It seemed she was doomed to butt heads with him today. What was he even doing here?

"Sit," Dr. Hartwood said. She was now done with her call and was seated in her swivel chair behind the desk.

"I hope I'm not interrupting anything," Alicia said, with a glance at Dr. GQ. "Would you like me to come back later?"

"No, it's fine," Dr. Hartwood said.

Alicia pulled back the available chair and sat down. A woody mint scent wafted into her nostrils, and Alicia stifled a groan. Anyone who was close to her knew she had a weakness for mint; this was definitely dangerous territory. *Get it together, Alicia. A man's scent does not tell you the kind of man he is*, a small voice told her.

She swallowed and forced her attention back on Dr. Hartwood.

"I'm disappointed that you were late for the ward round, Alicia." The professor cast a disapproving glance at her.

How did the professor know her first name? Calling her by it indicated they had some sort of relationship or familiarity which Alicia couldn't recall. And she would have remembered—there was no way she could have forgotten a fellow neat freak. Every book in the room had its place either on the shelf or on the professor's desk. She could see that the journals had been perused more than once—there were symmetrical color-coded sticky tabs adorning each one. Definitely a woman after her own heart.

"I had heard great things about you from Professor Smith, so I was a bit surprised," Dr. Hartwood continued.

Now everything made sense. Professor Smith was Alicia's attending on her last rotation in the Cardiology Service. Internal medicine residents like Alicia were expected to complete compulsory in-patient rotations in General Medicine, Cardiology, and ICU services, in addition to any other electives they might select. Alicia had enjoyed the rotation so much that she could have selected Cardiology as her fellowship of choice once she was done with the residency program. But she'd already set her heart on a Pulmonary and Critical Care fellowship. Dr. Smith had been disappointed but had understood.

Alicia gave the professor an apologetic smile. "It wasn't my intention. I had an emergency. But I should have notified my attending ahead of time. It won't happen again." She turned her head and glared at Dr. GQ, who was sitting in the chair next to hers. He only arched an eyebrow in response and gave her a faint smile which stirred something in her that had been dormant for many years.

I can't be attracted to him! she chided herself. This guy was her enemy—he'd already wrecked her day—and she had no business thinking about him in any other way beyond that.

"But that's not why I called you here," Dr. Hartwood said. "As you may be aware, the Annual Resident Research Symposium organized by the department is taking place this Friday. It's a great opportunity for fellows and residents to showcase their interest and commitment to medical research. You attended the one from last year, correct?"

Alicia nodded. She'd enjoyed listening to all the speakers, and it had been a great eye opener for her. In fact, it was through the symposium that she'd met Dr. Kim, a professor of Medical Genetics, and gotten the part-time research opportunity with him.

"We had one at my previous hospital, but I

suppose it would be different from the one here," Dr. GQ said.

Alicia's heart raced as his smooth voice assaulted her senses. It tickled and melted her insides, and her fists unclenched of their own volition. *Get a grip, Alicia!* she thought. She was supposed to be angry with him, not feeling tingling sensations at his closeness.

"Since Blake hasn't attended one here, I'll just explain how it works," Dr. Hartwood said as she leaned back in her grey swivel chair and twirled a pen between her fingers.

So his first name was Blake—it had a nice ring to it. But it didn't mean she liked him as a person. It seemed the professor was familiar with him. Maybe that was why it had been easy for him to transfer to Dexington Medical Center. Alicia stole a glance at him from the corner of her eye and noted he was studying his fingers like he found the whole discussion tedious. What was he doing here anyway? He could leave if he was that bored.

"The Annual Resident Research Symposium is the department's most important academic event of the year." The professor's words intruded on Alicia's thoughts. "Each internal medicine subspecialty is expected to forward the names of two speakers to represent them; the selection is made months in advance. The committee in charge of the symposium then decides which of those research presentations get a chance to present in an oral plenary session in front of the hospital medical staff; the remaining would put together poster presentations. All the speakers for this year's symposium have already been selected.

"However, this month is National Marrow Awareness Month," she continued. "The hospital has chosen to celebrate it this week and plans to hold a gala this Saturday to commemorate the event and raise funds for bone marrow research. So the department has decided to add one more speaker to the oral plenary roster to bring light to bone marrow research."

Alicia tucked her errant hair behind her ear. Why was the professor telling them this?

The professor dropped the pen, leaned forward, and steepled her fingers. "Each of you was recommended to be a speaker for this topic. Alicia, for your research with Dr. Kim on personal genomics, and Blake, for your research on leukemia. We noted that your research has both touched on the importance of bone marrow analysis as a bedrock for future treatment. The symposium committee couldn't come to an agreement on which one of you should take the spot, so we've decided that you'll both work together to make the presentation."

Alicia froze. She? Chosen to present? Unbelievable! She'd resigned herself to waiting until next year for a chance to present since fellows and third year residents were typically picked. She had expressed the same to Dr. Kim when he'd mentioned that their research looked promising enough to be selected. This was such a big deal. A grin split her face. But wait. Did Dr. Hartwood just say "work together"? With him? The guy who made a fool of her? She admired Dr. Hartwood, but there was no way she was going to work with this guy. It was just plain wrong.

She turned her face to glare at Blake, all traces of her smile gone. Definitely not happening!

CHAPTER 9

*B*lake had been surprised to see Dr. Montgomery walk into Dr. Hartwood's office and had been even more so when the professor had asked her to grab a seat. What was his father thinking? And how was she connected? The only way to find out was to hear what Dr. Hartwood had to say, so he settled into his chair and waited.

But he hadn't expected to find out he would be speaking at the symposium. Being selected was a big deal, something that most people worked round the year to prepare for. His face creased into a smile as he thought about the opportunity. But what did that have to do with the work for his father? He couldn't see the connection.

"Why do I have to work with him?" Alicia protested.

Blake's jaw muscle twitched, and he crossed his arms over his chest. This resident, Alicia—he liked her name, not that it mattered in the grand scheme of things—was now beginning to get on his nerves a little. What was the matter with her? It wasn't like he knew her from Adam. *What's with the attitude?* he wondered.

For some reason he couldn't hold back. "I don't recall falling over myself to work with you either," he said.

She shot him an angry look and opened her mouth to speak, but Dr. Hartwood halted their protests with a wave of her hand. "Alicia, are you aware that ten-thousand-dollar cash awards will be given to the best two presentations for the day?"

Blake watched with fascination at the speed at which Alicia's kissable lips clamped shut—it seemed money was a big deal for her. Wait. Why was he thinking about her lips? *Focus, Blake,* he thought.

"Ten thousand?" Alicia asked. Blake watched

her face become animated. "Do we both get ten thousand dollars or are we expected to split it if we win?"

He was right. She liked the money.

"You would each get that if you win—and that's a big IF considering the quality of research that would be presented—but only if you both end up on stage. If only one person represents you both and you win, you have to split it so you each get five thousand dollars. This is also a great opportunity to gain exposure and network with some of the best minds in the field who we've invited from other institutions for the symposium."

Blake watched Alicia push her chin upward. *I guess she wants the full cash award,* he thought, which meant he was in for a co-presentation.

Dr. Hartwood turned to Blake as she began twirling the pen again. "Blake, just so you know, your father insisted that you join this presentation. 'For visibility', he said."

Aha! So this would serve as the platform for his official introduction to the hospital leadership. Interesting.

Alicia stiffened. "What do you mean, his father?"

Time for the big reveal. He wondered how she would react.

Dr. Hartwood stopped spinning her pen. "Don't you know who Blake is? I'm sure you must have crossed paths during the residency interviews."

Blake couldn't recall ever seeing her before today's ward round. He would have noticed her spitfire personality immediately.

Alicia looked back and forth between Blake and the professor. "I don't understand," she said.

"His father is Phillip Dexington, as in Dexington Medical Center," Dr. Hartwood said.

If there were flies in the hospital, they would have had a heyday with the way Alicia's mouth dropped and stayed open.

CHAPTER 10

Alicia quickly recovered and closed her mouth. She couldn't believe what she'd just heard. She pointed a finger at Blake. "You mean his family owns this hospital?"

"Hello, I'm right here." Blake waved his hands in front of Alicia.

"Yes," Dr. Hartwood replied.

Alicia slumped into her seat. No wonder the guy had treated her in such a cavalier manner. She thought the day had been bad enough, but it seemed her week just got worse. How did she end up in this situation with a spoiled brat? *Another guy who thinks his status and connection is everything.* She'd met enough of them in her lifetime and disliked them with a passion—they'd all felt they could do anything and get away with it. No wonder he wasn't even concerned that he had splashed mud on her. But he had another think coming if he thought he could get away with it.

"From what I've heard about you both, I'm sure you can pull together something wonderful on such short notice. I'm counting on you, and I'm looking forward to seeing your presentation slides. Can I trust you both to do a good job?" The professor looked hard at both of them.

"Yes we can," Blake said.

"Yes," Alicia said. Well, they would have to co-present. The option for either of them to present alone didn't exist as far as she was concerned, especially with the extra ten thousand dollars hanging in the balance. And there was no way she was going to let him take all the spotlight. She needed this money like she needed air. It was a miracle staring her in the face. That was Willow's treatment money right there, and she would make this presentation the best she had ever put together and make sure she got every single dime.

"Good," Dr. Hartwood said. "My secretary will give you both a packet of the previous year's presentations so you can use that as a guide to see what we are expecting from you. Now leave my office and go do whatever you residents usually do," the professor said.

With a quick wave of her hand, the professor shooed them out of her office.

Alicia and Blake stepped out of Dr. Hartwood's office and stopped by the secretary's desk on their way out.

"Here you go." The secretary gave them a quick smile and handed them each a packet.

"Thanks," Alicia responded. She saw Blake flash a lazy smile at the secretary.

Jerk. Alicia didn't know why she was bothered by his smile, but she was upset nevertheless. She stalked by him out of the secretary's office and into the hallway.

"Now you have to tell me what's wrong." Alicia felt a hand on her arm and turned to see Blake standing behind her. The woody mint scent emanating from him caused her heart to pick up its pace and her skin to tingle. She jerked away her arm and felt the loss of his warm skin immediately.

"You really don't know?" she said.

"I don't. I wouldn't be asking if I did. And it's not like we've met before."

Alicia had been about to remind him about the splashing incident, but the latter part of his comment stopped her cold. How could he forget so easily what had happened earlier today? It had ruined her morning, and yet it had not been a blip on his radar? For some reason, it rankled her. Her blood boiled, and she could feel the pressure of the smoke threatening to escape from her ears. She needed to part ways with him soon or she might just blow up. "You know what? Save it. Let's just split the work."

It looked like he'd been about to say something but then changed his mind.

She leaned against the wall in the hallway and flipped through the contents of the packet she'd been given. After a minute, she closed them and placed it back in the envelope. "I think we need to focus on four main sections. We could start with an overview of bone marrow analysis, followed by how it has been used in the past. Then the current thinking in personal genomics, and how bone marrow analysis factors into it. And then finish with the future application ideas and ongoing research about the role of bone marrow analysis in the treatment of genetic disease and genetic-related cancers, using the personal genomics approach."

Blake nodded. "I think that's fine. I'll take number four."

Alicia raised an eyebrow. "Okay, but I expect number four to be very comprehensive."

Blake flashed a smile. "Oh, it will be. You don't have to worry."

His smile caught her off-guard and made her stomach quiver. Alicia tucked her hair behind her ear.

"Can I have your number?" Blake asked. He pulled his phone from his coat pocket.

"What?" Was this the new pickup line? Well, it wouldn't work on her.

"Your number. I need to be able to reach you if I have any questions."

Oh. Heat crept up her neck. She called out the digits, which he tapped into his phone.

Her phone beeped in her pocket.

"That's my number," he said. "Make sure you save it."

"Whatever." Alicia stood away from the wall and turned to walk away. "I'll let you know this evening where we'll meet tomorrow. We don't have much time before Friday."

"Works for me," Blake said. "Let me know when you have everything set up."

Alicia didn't respond and stalked off. So, he expected her to be responsible for everything. She would deliver, but he'd better do the same.

Because she had no plans to carry dead weight along.

CHAPTER 11

Alicia stepped through the foyer of the Victorian brownstone that she shared with her two roommates, Dana Adams and Jasmine Banks. She loved coming home to this place—it was nestled in a quiet tree-lined street in one of the older sections of the city and was about ten minutes away from the hospital. Jasmine had advertised for a roommate on the internal online board the hospital created for incoming residents, and Alicia had responded to the ad.

The apartment had been a steal to rent. It turned out the place belonged to Jasmine's aunt, and Jasmine and Dana were already roommates. Alicia had met up with them a week before orientation and they had hit it off, which was surprising since Alicia didn't make friends easily. Jasmine was now a third-year obstetrics and gynecology resident, while Dana was a fourth-year general surgical resident.

"Hey, you're back," Dana said. A petite beauty with blond hair and gorgeous blue eyes, Dana had an innocence that the hard knocks of life hadn't managed to change. She sat on the couch in the living room that boasted grand bay windows, a fireplace, crown molding, and a winding staircase that led to the upper floors, and which shared an open concept floor plan with the dining space and kitchen. Alicia knew without looking that Dana was watching a rerun of her favorite soap opera.

"What's wrong?" Dana asked, searching Alicia's face. Alicia dropped her bag on the dining table and let out a big sigh.

"I just had a really tough day," she responded. "I'm upset just thinking about it."

"That's a first. Spill," Jasmine said as she peered over the coffee table.

Alicia startled. "You scared me! I didn't know you were there."

Jasmine grinned. "Sorry." Her pearly whites

glowed in contrast with her gorgeous red hair. She was lying on the area rug with her arms resting on a pillow. Alicia was pretty sure that Jasmine had just finished another workout session—as evidenced by the sweat-stained tank top and yoga pants.

Alicia flopped down on the couch and told them what had happened with the red car driver, how he'd turned out to be Blake Dexington, and how she now had to prepare a presentation with him.

"You mean Blake Dexington, aka the hottest guy in our lovely town?" Dana asked.

"Do you know him?"

Jasmine and Dana looked at each other and burst out laughing.

"What's funny?"

"Alicia, the question should be, why don't you know him?" Jasmine said.

"Hmmm. He's that popular?"

"Not popular. I would say mysterious," Jasmine said.

"Yes, mysterious," Dana echoed. "He's very friendly, but also a bit aloof from women; you can tell he doesn't want any entanglements. And

I can assure you that many have tried, and I don't blame them."

"He is definitely cute and generally well-mannered, so this behavior of his you've told us about seems kind of strange," Jasmine agreed. "And I've never seen you so upset about a guy. Are you sure you don't like him?" she teased Alicia.

Alicia's face grew warm. "No way!" she responded.

"She is blushing," Dana said.

"Alicia never blushes. Oh my, you must really like this guy," Jasmine said.

"I don't!" Alicia countered. "Oh, stop it!"

"But isn't he hot?" Jasmine asked.

"Well, he is kinda," Alicia responded. "But he is an insufferable pig with cute dimples."

Dana and Jasmine exchanged glances and laughed. "She noticed the dimples," Dana said to Jasmine.

"Alicia is definitely in the like zone," Jasmine responded, nodding her head. Turning to Alicia, "And he likes you?" she asked.

"Why would he?" Alicia responded.

"Well, if he asked for your number ..." Dana said.

"It's only for the presentation."

"Really?" Dana and Jasmine both echoed in unison.

"Oh, you ladies are unreasonable. I can't even …." Alicia got up to head toward the stairs that led to her room.

"You wait and see, Mrs. Alicia Dexington," quipped Jasmine.

Alicia grabbed a pillow from the couch and threw it at Jasmine's head. She missed, and the pillow hit the TV instead. She could hear Jasmine's laughter echoing after her even as she walked up the stairs and headed to her room on the second floor. Jasmine occupied the master suite on the first floor, while Dana and Alicia had separate bedrooms on the second floor.

Alicia entered her room and collapsed on the edge of her bed.

Alicia Dexington. It had a nice ring to it. Wait. What was she thinking? Alicia shook her head. There was no way she could have anything with someone like Blake, even if he turned out to be different like Jasmine had suggested. If only her roommates knew that love wasn't in the future for her. She just needed to focus on Willow and her treatment.

Alicia rubbed her temples. She could feel the beginnings of a headache coming on.

Maybe a quick nap would help her feel better.

Alicia yawned and stretched her limbs. She had felt better after the nap and had spent the last four hours at her desk working on the presentation. And she was happy with what she had pulled together. Getting the materials to use hadn't been too difficult, and she had reached out to Dr. Kim, who had also sent some helpful documents her way.

Alicia adjusted the frame of her oversized glasses on her nose, leaned forward, and pulled her window curtain aside. It was already dark outside, but she could still make out the cobblestone sidewalks, the decorative iron work that fenced the front yards, and the parked cars, all made visible by gas streetlamps. The weather was nice for a walk outside, but she was waiting to hear back from the administrative coordinator about conference room availability at the hospital.

Alicia needed a room with a projector to walk through the draft presentation with Blake tomorrow, so a coffee shop was out of the question. None had been available for the rest of the week via the online scheduler, but she was aware that the administrative coordinator sometimes secured blocks of time for emergency purposes. Alicia had reached out to her. The administrative coordinator had said she would get back to her today on any available space. Alicia expected her email at any time. She needed to let Blake know where they would be meeting tomorrow as she had promised.

She let the curtain drop back into place and moved from the desk to her bed.

Blake. The mere thought of him twisted her insides all up. She had been angry at him, but he'd deserved it. But that didn't mean she couldn't be civil with him the next time they met. After all, they had no choice but to work together. And Jasmine's comment had reminded her that you can't judge a book by its cover. She would give him another chance.

She tucked her hair behind her ear. But why had she been so bothered by him? It was really unlike her. Many people had wronged her even worse than he'd done, and she'd never batted an eyelid. Why him? "It's nothing," she told herself. It definitely wasn't what Jasmine and Dana were suggesting.

There was no way that she liked him. Jasmine and Dana must have been high on something. It was impossible, and moreover, there was no room in her life for love. The last time she'd opened her heart, she had paid dearly for it.

Another heartbreak like that would kill her.

CHAPTER 12

*A*licia's phone beeped. She reached out and grabbed it from her desk. It was an email from the administrative coordinator letting her know that no conference room was available. She dropped her phone on her bed. This wasn't good.

Alicia ran her hand through her hair. *Aargh.* This had been her last option. Where would she find a conference room now? She'd even called hotels in the area, but their meeting rooms were fully booked for the next few months. She flopped back on the bed. She had to let Blake know—two heads were better than one. Maybe they could come up with a workable solution together. She grabbed her phone and sent him a quick text.

Her phone pinged. *That was fast*, Alicia mused as she picked up her phone to read the screen.

Blake: We can use my apartment. I have a projector in my home office.

Alicia's face grew warm. His apartment? Was he kidding? That had danger written all over it.

Alicia: I don't think that's a good idea.

Blake: Do you have any other suggestions?

Alicia: Hmmm. What about the call room? There's a projector there.

Blake: If you are okay with a place that stinks of sweat and stale food.

Alicia wrinkled her nose. Definitely not a good option.

Blake: My place is fine. We are both adults, and nothing will happen.

Alicia leaned back on her headboard. Could she take the risk? His place seemed like the only option available at such short notice. But was it really safe? Alicia hadn't forgotten the horror stories of girls who'd been date raped—she'd seen young ladies wake up in the ER only to find out they had been slipped a roofie. One couldn't be too careful these days. This wasn't even a date, and she didn't really know him. What if he tried something funny?

She got off her bed and paced in front of it in her pink ducky slippers. "I think it will be okay," she said to herself as she adjusted her oversized glasses on her nose. She had attended numerous self-defense classes and had some martial arts training under her belt. She could defend herself if it came to it.

Alicia: Okay I'll see you at six p.m. tomorrow.

Blake: Sounds good.

Another ping. Alicia looked at the screen. Blake had sent her his address.

It was now set in stone. She would find out tomorrow what kind of person Blake was.

But she was going armed with her pepper spray just in case.

CHAPTER 13

*B*lake tugged at his polo shirt and looked again at the time on the wall clock. Alicia would be here any minute. He didn't know why, but he'd been in a good mood all day. Even his best friend, Josh—who was a surgical resident and who he'd had lunch with—had commented that he'd had a perpetual grin on his face.

Blake had never let a woman into his apartment before. Well, except for his mother, and she'd only visited the first time he'd moved in. He considered it too personal. He'd been surprised at his willingness to invite her over; it had seemed as natural as breathing air.

His phone rang. It was the concierge,

informing him that a certain Dr. Montgomery had arrived to see him. Blake thanked him and padded over to the doorbell camera to activate the code that allowed his private elevator to open on the ground floor. He watched her for the entire elevator ride. *Gosh, she's beautiful*, he thought. *Guard your heart, Blake.* He put in another code, and the elevator doors opened to reveal the dark-haired beauty who had invaded his thoughts—despite his resistance—standing before him. His heart picked up its rhythm.

"Hi, come on in," he said. She was dressed in a simple light-pink top and blue jeans, but the combination seemed to accentuate rather than diminish her beauty.

"Thanks," she responded. She stepped in and looked around. "You have a beautiful home," she said.

"Thanks," Blake said.

The ensuing silence was uncomfortable— a first for Blake, since he always knew what to say to the ladies.

"The projector?" she asked.

"Oh, yes … this way."

Blake led her to his study. He'd already engaged the projector, and it jutted from the ceiling. A laptop sat on an exotic wooden round table that stood off on one side of the room in front of matching bookshelves that lined every corner and wall in the office. Alicia pulled out a custom leather seat from the table, while Blake grabbed another.

She removed her leather tote from where it hung on her shoulder and placed it on the table. "Why don't I show you what I have, and then you can share what you've put together?" she said.

"That's fine. But before we get started, I think it's important we clear the air," Blake said.

A pair of gorgeous brown eyes studied him while she waited for him to speak.

Blake swallowed. For some reason, he felt like a schoolboy about to ask the girl he liked out for the first time. "I think I may have offended you in some way, but I don't know how. Do you think you could tell me what happened?"

Alicia hesitated for a moment and tucked a piece of her hair behind her ear. Then she told him what had happened yesterday.

Blake felt like a fool. No wonder she'd been hostile to him. And Alicia had been the banshee he'd encountered! It had never crossed his mind she could be the same person sitting across from him right now. There was only one choice—he needed to make things right.

"I apologize, Alicia. I had no idea I splashed water on you, and it wasn't my intention to cast you in a bad light before the professor. I can't even imagine how you must have felt yesterday."

He saw what looked like an incredulous look cross her face briefly before it disappeared. "That's okay. Now that I think about it, I may have overreacted a bit."

He gave a small smile. "Do you think we can put it behind us?"

She smiled back in return. "Sounds good."

Blake felt light-hearted, like a weight had been lifted off his shoulders. He'd underestimated how much he wanted things to be good between them. "Great! So let me introduce myself. Hi, I'm Blake Dexington. Nice to meet you." He extended his hand to her.

She hesitated for a moment and then shook his hand. "Alicia Montgomery."

"Okay, now we can get down to business."

Alicia opened her bag and pulled out a USB

drive. "May I?" she asked, gesturing at the laptop.

"Yes, go right ahead."

She leaned forward and plugged the USB drive into the side of the laptop. A folder window popped open on the screen. She double-clicked on the file icon shown in the folder, and a PowerPoint document filled the screens of both the laptop and the projector.

For the next hour, Blake listened intently as Alicia talked through the presentation slides she had prepared. He interrupted her at intervals to ask a few clarifying questions, which Alicia was quick to address. She noted any changes required in a text box on the slides.

She's really good, Blake thought. He'd learned so much just in this short period of time, and it was clear she was passionate about the topic. He'd figured she was smart, but she had blown his expectations out of the water.

"Nice work," he said, once she'd come to the end of her presentation. "When did you even have time to pull this all together?"

"Thanks," she responded. Her face might have turned a light shade of pink, but Blake wasn't sure.

He leaned back in his seat and stretched his arms. "How about we take a short break and come back to it? I haven't eaten anything since breakfast."

"I'm not hungry," she said. Her stomach growled in response, and Blake could see her ears turn pink.

He stifled a grin and tried to keep his face blank. "I made dinner."

Her eyebrows rose. "Made it or ordered it?" she asked.

"Come see for yourself." He rose and led the way to the kitchen. It was his favorite room in the apartment and featured walls bathed in soft grey, dark granite countertops, cherry cabinets, and top-of-the-line Miele kitchen appliances that would make any chef envious. The faint smell of pine lingered in the air. Blake walked over to the oven, opened it, and pulled out a pan with whole braised fish resting in a sauce and covered with sprinkles of thin-sliced scallions and cucumber. The smells of garlic and ginger followed it.

Alicia sat on one of the kitchen bar stools and leaned against the countertop. "That smells delicious. Did you braise the fish yourself?" she asked.

"I sure did. I actually love cooking. It's a great way to unwind after a stressful day." Alicia made a face. "I guess cooking isn't your thing," he said.

"How did you know? Let's just say you don't want me near the kitchen."

Blake laughed. "That bad, eh?" She smiled and said nothing. Blake couldn't believe how natural it felt having her in his kitchen and talking about food with her. *Be careful, Blake,* he thought. It could become addicting.

"So how do you unwind?" he asked, as he pulled out two plates from the plate-warming cabinet in front of him.

"I like to take walks. Something about breathing in and exhaling the fresh air helps me a lot." Blake nodded. Unwinding at the end of the day was critical in their chosen profession. Most people thought it was easy for doctors to stomach what they saw daily, but doctors needed to let down their hair so to speak, for the sake of their mental health. "I also like watching Korean dramas," she said.

Blake raised an eyebrow. "Korean dramas?"

"Don't look so shocked. A lot of people enjoy them, so most of them are subtitled. A lot of their dramas are light, fun, and sometimes hilarious, perfect for taking my mind away from all the life and death issues."

"Hmmm. I've never watched one before. Maybe I'll try it someday."

"They do have some that are more action-packed, or thrillers, if that's more your speed." He noticed Alicia's eyes on him as he brought out two sets of cutlery from a cabinet drawer. "So who taught you how to cook?" she asked.

He dished out the fish onto the plates and placed one in front of her with a set of cutlery. "My mother. She taught us how to take care of ourselves. What would you like to drink?"

"Water is fine. She must be special."

"She is." Blake grew quiet. He hadn't really thought about his mother for quite some time. He would call her tomorrow.

Alicia said nothing, and the silence soon became a bit uncomfortable. To distract himself, Blake filled two glasses with water from the sink and handed one to Alicia. Then he picked up a remote on a far corner of the kitchen counter and pressed the ON button. The vibrant sound of a classical music-with-beats instrumental filled the room.

Alicia lifted an eyebrow. "Interesting choice. I wouldn't have pegged you as liking this kind of music."

Blake shrugged. "It's fun. It's like mixing the old with the new. What sort of music do you like?"

"I like classical—my favorite is Mozart. I know he has a lot of haters, but I love his music. How do I describe it? It doesn't have its nose bent out of shape."

Blake chuckled. "That's an interesting way to put it. Have you been to any concerts that featured his music?"

"Once. I went to a concert at the Boston Symphony Hall while I was a medical student. Even though I sat so far away from center stage that I could barely see the orchestra, the music swirled around the whole hall. It was glorious."

Blake was intrigued by how animated Alicia's face became as she spoke. Clearly one of her passions. He grabbed a bar stool and sat across from her with his own plate in front of him. "Bon appétit," he said.

"Thank you," she said quietly and then bent

her head. Blake figured she was praying. He waited till she was done, and then they both ate in silence.

"This is so good," she finally said.

"Thanks. What's your favorite food?" he asked.

"You'll laugh at me." A smile tugged at the corner of her lips. Blake had to tear his eyes away from those inviting lips.

"No, I won't." He tried to keep a straight face, but wasn't successful.

"See, you are already laughing!"

Blake chuckled. "Okay, okay, I'll stop. Now I'm serious. See my serious face? Go ahead. Tell me."

Alicia looked at her hands. She seemed to struggle a bit before responding. "It's a home-made pancake with a smiley face written in chocolate syrup." Blake burst out laughing, and Alicia covered her face with her hands. "See, I knew you would laugh."

"Sorry." He tried to keep his mirth in, but it was a struggle.

"My mom made it for me before she passed away." A fleeting moment of pain crossed her eyes.

Blake winced. He shouldn't have been laughing. Before he could apologize, she spoke up. "What's your favorite?" she asked.

"Fish and chips." he said. "But I haven't had it in years." His mood grew pensive. Thinking about fish and chips made him recall the past, memories he preferred to tuck away.

He looked up to see Alicia staring straight into his eyes. Like she knew how he felt. The air felt thick with emotion. Blake scrambled for what to say to clear the air, but Alicia beat him to it.

"Have you seen the new patient admitted this afternoon in ward C?" she said.

"You mean Mr. Pilensky?" Blake responded.

"Yes."

"Not yet."

"Don't go and see him." Alicia seemed to struggle to keep a straight face.

"What do you …? Did something happen?"

"Well, I went to the ward after the grand round this afternoon to see if there were any new patients admitted and noticed his name on the nurses' board. He's not my patient, but I thought his case was interesting and asked one of the nurses at the station if it was a good time to chat with him. She exchanged quick glances with another nurse, but said it was okay. I didn't think anything of it."

By now, Alicia had finished her food and settled in comfortably. Blake was curious to see how the story would unfold.

"I walked into Ward C and noticed that the beds next to his were empty, but I didn't really register what it meant. Mr. Pilensky was lying down on his bed in the far corner of the room. I asked him if this was a good time to chat with him. Mr. Pilensky responded by tooting."

"Tooting?" Blake asked, confusion written all over his face.

"Tooting gas." It now dawned on Blake what she'd meant, and he had to force himself to hold back the laughter.

"Each time I repeated the question, the response grew bigger and louder. And he had this look of ecstasy on his face with each release. Like he was in toot heaven. I realized that if I stayed there any longer, I might just die of gas poisoning," Alicia continued. By this time, Blake was hollering in laughter. "Can you imagine the headline: 'Doctor dies of toot gas'?"

It took all of Blake's restraint not to roll on the floor with laughter.

"I didn't know when I ran out to the hallway, gasping for fresh air," Alicia continued. By now, Blake was guffawing and clutched his midsection. "Once the nurses saw me, they burst out laughing. Now I understood why the beds beside him were empty. I mean, who wants to come into the hospital and then die from secondhand bodily gas eruptions?"

"Did you go back in again?"

Alicia shot him a glance. "I don't have a death wish."

Blake erupted again in laughter. He'd never laughed so much. His insides felt like they would fall out any moment. He had no idea Alicia could be this funny and easy to talk to, and he loved seeing this side of her. "You'll love my grandmother," he said. "She's just as hilarious as you are." Alicia kept smiling at him. "What?"

"You look so different when you laugh. It's nice to see," she said.

Then Blake realized she'd tried to change his mood, even at the expense of laughing at herself. His heart flipped. And at that moment,

Blake knew something had changed forever between them.

The air grew warm and comfortable. It was a strange feeling, but he could have stayed like that with her all day. However, it was getting late.

He would dwell later on what had happened tonight. For now, they needed to finish up the presentation.

CHAPTER 14

Blake presented his piece for the next thirty minutes.

"This is really good," Alicia commented. It was clear from the look on her face that she was surprised. "How did you get all this information?"

Blake shrugged and smiled. "It's a secret," he said.

"Alright. Let's talk through all the changes we need to make to be sure we are on the same page," Alicia said. They spent the next fifteen minutes discussing the adjustments that would make the presentation tighter. Blake found he enjoyed the back-and-forth conversation and loved Alicia's ideas.

"I think we can stop here for tonight," Alicia said. "Why don't you send me your revised slides tomorrow morning? I don't believe the changes will be that hard to incorporate. I'll update mine as well and pull both into a single deck. We can do a final walkthrough tomorrow evening,"

"Same time?" Blake felt an adrenaline rush at the thought of seeing her again.

"Sure."

"Can I drop you off at home since it's very late?"

"I'll just take the bus," Alicia responded a bit too quickly.

Hmmm. Maybe she still felt uncomfortable around him, which was fine. It wasn't like they knew each other very well yet. Blake led her through the foyer, and they took the elevator to the lobby.

"I'll walk you to the bus stop," Blake offered.

Alicia hesitated for a moment, but then gave a quick nod.

The night air was cool and breezy as they strolled down the sidewalk. There were not very many people on the streets; most residents— young professionals—were either on their way home from work or probably indoors by now since it was a weekday. The streets would look very different once Friday rolled by.

Walking with Alicia felt like something Blake had done before and wanted to do again. He cut a quick glance at her. She clutched her tote as a shield against her body and looked lost in thought. The bus stop was just up ahead and stood empty.

A loud sound behind him caught his attention. He turned and watched in horror as a motorcycle careened right toward Alicia!

Alicia felt hands grab her out of the way and twirl her into a strong embrace. She looked up to see herself in Blake's arms. Warm. Safe. Those were the words that popped into her mind. A part of her wanted to savor the feeling, but she quickly came to her senses.

"Are you okay?" She heard the panic in his voice.

"What? Yes, I'm fine." Alicia stepped away from him and tucked a piece of her hair behind her ear. "Why?"

"You almost got hit by a motorcycle!"

"What? Really? I…" Alicia looked behind her and saw the taillight of a motorbike disappearing into the night. "Thank you for saving me." She looked down. She wasn't standing on the road. "But why was he on the sidewalk?"

"I don't know, and I can't imagine why. He didn't even bother to stop. Unfortunately, I couldn't catch his license plate number. I still think we should report it."

"Wait … No, don't do that. I'm okay. It's no big deal."

"But you could have been hurt!"

"But I wasn't." Alicia wrapped her arms around herself. "Could we drop it?" Though Blake didn't know it, Alicia didn't like talking to the cops. She had already had her fill of them when they came to deliver the news about her sister's death. In her mind, cops equaled bad news.

Blake had a grim look on his face, and his lips were pressed into a thin line. Alicia reached out a hand and touched his arm. "Thank you for saving me," she said softly.

Blake let out a deep sigh and raked his hand through his hair.

"Can I drop you at home now?" Blake asked.

"I'm fine. See, the bus is here." Alicia

stepped away and headed toward the bus that had just arrived.

"Call me when you get home," Blake called out.

Alicia gave a quick wave over her head and stepped into the bus.

When Alicia entered her apartment, there was no one else at home. It wasn't hard to imagine where Jasmine and Dana were. The residency life was too busy to allow for much else. She headed to her room, dropped her bag on her desk, and crashed on her bed. It had been a long day, and every part of her body ached.

But she wasn't yet done for the evening. Alicia pulled out her tablet from her tote and accessed the hospital's Electronic Medical Records. There were new notes in the EMR that had been signed for her patients, and Alicia put in a few orders. Four new patients had also been admitted so far for her team, so she read up on them in anticipation of the next day. She signed out of the system and tossed her tablet on her desk. Now she could turn in for the night.

She'd promised Blake she'd let him know when she got home, so she pulled out her phone and sent him a quick text. Her phone rang instead, and Alicia picked it up. "Hi, Blake."

"Hey. I'm glad you got home safely. You gave me quite a scare earlier."

"Thanks again."

"No worries. Thank you for the laughs. I enjoyed dinner with you."

"You know it wasn't a date, right?" Alicia slammed her hand over her mouth. She really should be more careful. It seemed being around Blake loosened some of her inhibitions. "Not that I'm fishing for a date," she corrected.

Blake chuckled. "Definitely not a date."

"Alright. Have a wonderful night."

"Good night, Alicia." The sound of her name from his lips made her feel all warm and fuzzy on the inside.

"Good night, Blake." She pressed the end call button.

What a day. Wait, she was still smiling. It was as if she could still feel his arms around her and hear the concern in his voice.

Alicia hadn't expected the evening to turn out the way it had. She'd gone armed with pepper spray and had come out with a different impression of Blake. Jasmine had been right. He was not at all like the entitled rich boy persona she had pegged him with. She could tell he was just being himself, and she'd liked what she'd seen. She'd felt so at ease with him, like they'd known each other forever. Alicia couldn't kid herself—she had enjoyed the attention and the conversations.

But that didn't mean there could be anything more than friendship between them. "Alicia, this is all a mirage," she told herself. Besides, if he knew the real her, he would probably take off and never come back. There was no way she could ever be in a relationship with a man like him.

But their interaction this evening had been a breath of fresh air, like a delicious treat she hadn't realized she'd been missing out on. And she wanted more of it as long as she could.

Alicia placed her arms under her head. So, this was what she was going to do—she would enjoy the time she spent with him while they worked on the presentation together. She could allow herself that, and then go back to her old life when it was all over. Yes, that she could do.

Alicia changed into her nightclothes, washed her face, and climbed into bed.

Thoughts of Blake were still on her mind as she drifted off into sleep.

CHAPTER 16

The next morning, Alicia's footsteps clicked on the tiled floors as she made her way to the conference room for the morning report. The morning report was a mandatory daily conference for residents, during which an attending would lead an interactive discussion on a recent interesting case that had been admitted.

Alicia was relieved that the patient of interest today wasn't hers—she had been up since the early hours of the morning working on the presentation before heading to the wards to review the sign out from the night team and lead a pre-round with her team for all the patients they now covered, including seven new patients. Even Mrs. Carter looked more peaceful —the grief counseling must have been good for her—before she had been moved to the surgical unit.

Alicia quickened her steps till she got to the open doorway of the conference room. Most of her fellow residents were already seated around the long table. Her eyes swept the room for an unoccupied spot—turned out the only one available was next to Blake, and he had his head bent over the tablet in front of him. A thrill buzzed through her veins at seeing him, but she ignored it. She made her way to the empty seat and cleared her throat.

Blake looked up at the interruption, and a smile grazed his face. Alicia's heart leaped. She gave him a small smile back. "Is this seat taken?" she asked.

"Not at all." If there was an award called 'Voice Most Likely to Turn Alicia's Insides Mushy', Blake would definitely win it.

Alicia pulled the seat and sat down. At that moment, the attending walked in and the morning report began.

One of her colleagues had admitted a patient with Hirschsprung's disease, a rare congenital gastrointestinal disorder that typically manifested in newborns. In this case, the patient had presented in adulthood with no previous history of gastrointestinal problems in earlier years.

Alicia listened with rapt attention as the attending discussed the main points of the case, with the direction of the chief resident. Before she knew it, she was exchanging ideas with Blake about the patient's disease. Conversing with him was easy, and Blake was far more knowledgeable than she'd given him credit for. He was really unlike other rich young men she had met.

Alicia noticed some of the other residents whispered and gave them curious looks. *We are not a couple,* she wanted to tell them. *But I think you wish you were,* her mind protested. Alicia felt her face grow warm. Shutting down that train of thought before it went elsewhere, she focused on what the attending was saying.

Soon enough the morning report came to an end. When it was over, Alicia turned to Blake. "That was interesting. Thanks for the running commentary."

"I never imagined the morning report could be this fun," Blake said. He smiled at her, and his eyes seemed to reach into her soul. It was like the rest of the world dropped away, and there were only the two of them in the room. She didn't even notice the other residents get up and leave the room.

"Ah…em," a voice spoke beside them.

Alicia broke eye contact with Blake and looked up behind her. A handsome-looking young man—probably of Spanish heritage—in green scrubs under a medical coat, looked down at her with curiosity in his eyes.

Blake's face broke into a smile. "Hey, Josh," said Blake. "Josh, this is …"

"Alicia Montgomery," Josh finished. "I know who she is. Nice to meet you, Alicia."

Alicia's eyes widened. She'd never met him before, so how did he know who she was? "Hello," she said.

"Josh is my best buddy," Blake said to Alicia. "We grew up together, and he is a surgical resident here at the hospital."

It still didn't explain how Josh knew her— she hadn't worked with him on any surgical consults either in the ward or in the ER. But this was her cue to leave. She had patients waiting for her. She got up. "Blake, I have to go. It was nice meeting you, Josh."

Blake stood up as well. "Okay, I'll see you tonight. Did you get the file I sent to you?"

"Yes. I'll pull them together later today, and we can talk through them tonight," Alicia said.

She gave them a brief smile and left the conference room.

CHAPTER 17

*B*lake stared at her back as she left, her ponytailed hair swinging from side to side.

"You like her," Josh said to Blake.

Blake scoffed. "What?"

"I know you, and you like her. I watched you for a while at the door before I came over. You should have seen your face. You couldn't tear your eyes away from her. But you did good— you chose one of the smartest cookies around here."

"What do you mean?"

"Her reputation precedes her. Top of her class at Harvard Medical School. Highest USMLE Step I & II scores of any resident in the hospital. She could have easily gotten into any program she wanted. I heard she was offered a spot here before the matching results even came out. I know a lot of male residents and fellows who have been trying to get close to her, but you, my friend, are the first to succeed."

Interesting. Blake knew Alicia was intelligent, but he didn't know she was that impressive.

"Good to know. But we are only working on a presentation together."

"Keep telling yourself that," Josh said with a smirk on his face.

Blake cuffed his head and headed for the door of the conference room.

"Ouch! What was that for?" Josh rubbed his head and hastened to catch up with Blake.

"To bring you to your senses," Blake retorted.

The rest of the day was so hectic that Alicia never thought it would come to an end. She was on day float duty and oversaw admissions to the wards. Alicia had forgotten how busy it could be. She had started off the day with six old patients and seven new ones, but had ended up with twenty patients so far with two discharged.

The attending round had been longer than usual given the number of new patients, but she had a good team of interns who'd kept up with them all. Together they had been able to finish the list of to-dos with enough time for her to teach and coach the medical student assigned to her team. So, it was a relief when she signed off at six p.m and handed the patients over to the night float team. She had just enough time to get home and take a shower before heading to Blake's place.

Alicia had finalized the presentation in the afternoon and had sent a copy to Dr. Kim to get his feedback. He'd been happy with what they had put together and had made some suggestions, which Alicia had incorporated.

Later that evening, Alicia and Blake met again in Blake's apartment to finish up the deck.

"I like what we've ended up with," Blake said once they had finished the run through. "Thank God it's done."

"Me too," Alicia said as she stretched her arms over her head.

"Would you like to send the presentation to the professor?"

"Sure. Done. I copied you and Dr. Kim on the email."

"Thanks. Would you like to stay for dinner?"

"I'm not really hungry." Alicia's stomach growled. Her face turned beet red. Why did this have to happen anytime she was with Blake?

But Blake only smiled. "I made pasta," he said.

Alicia's stomach growled again in response, and she covered her face with her hands. This was way too embarrassing.

Blake chuckled. "Let's go."

"This is really good. Do you cook a lot?" Alicia asked as she dug into the food.

"Whenever I can. It's very therapeutic," Blake responded.

Alicia couldn't help cleaning off her plate. The pasta and the sauce were that good.

"So, do you have any siblings?" Blake asked.

Alicia's fork stopped in midair. She put down the fork gently and rested both arms on the kitchen countertop. Emotions swirled within her like they always did when she thought about her sister. She took a deep breath. "I had one, Mary. She's dead."

"I'm sorry, I shouldn't have asked," Blake said gently.

"It's okay. Mary and her husband Kevin were killed three years ago in a car accident. They were hit by a drunk driver." Alicia had been in her final year in medical school when it happened. People said the pain would go away. But it never did, not really. Mary had not only been her sister but her best friend as well despite the age difference between them, and Alicia still missed her daily even after all this time. She gave Blake a tremulous smile.

Blake covered her right hand with his. It felt warm and comforting. "I'm sure you miss her," he said in a quiet tone. Tears pooled behind Alicia's eyes, and she kept her face down. She couldn't look at him for fear that the tears would spill over. By this time, Blake had moved from where he'd perched on a bar stool opposite her, and he now sat on the one next to her. He put his arm over her shoulders, drawing her close.

"I do," she said. Uttering those two words broke open a dam in Alicia, the same one that had stayed shut even when she had received the news that her sister was dead. Sobs racked her body, and tears streamed down her face.

Blake just kept rubbing her shoulder as she released pent-up tears that she didn't know she had in her. They kept coming down, and at one point Blake pressed a handkerchief into her hand. Eventually, she had no more to shed.

"I know how it feels losing someone close to you," Blake said.

Had he lost someone as well? But it wasn't her place to probe for details. He would tell her, if or when he was ready.

She used the handkerchief to wipe her face. "I'm so sorry. I didn't know I was going to be this emotional," she said. She could only imagine how awful she looked, and heat crept up her face.

"No worries. I'm sorry I made you cry," Blake responded.

They stayed quiet like that for some time, not speaking. It was pleasant. Alicia now felt lighter, like some weight had been lifted off. But who was this guy that touched places in her that she'd closed off to anyone else? After a few minutes, she spoke. "But my sister left me with the most precious gift in the world, my niece Willow."

"How old is she?"

"She is eight. She's the strongest, funniest person I've ever known." At Blake's inquiring look, "She suffers from cystic fibrosis," Alicia continued. "She's had lots of incidents, but she's a fighter. It was part of the reason why I chose to do my residency here at Dexington Medical Center. It has one of the best CF research programs in the country."

"Who takes care of her?" Blake asked.

"I do. She has spent most of her life in the hospital and is currently an inpatient here."

"I would love to meet her."

Alicia looked at Blake. His eyes were open and trusting. Maybe.

They stayed silent for a few more minutes. Then her phone pinged, and she looked at the screen. "It's an email from the professor." She swiped the screen and read the email. "She's happy with the deck and forwarded it to the symposium coordinator. She copied you and me on the email."

"That's great." Blake pulled his phone from his pocket and checked it. "I got the forwarded email. You know what? I'll make sure the presentation is all set up in the auditorium in the morning since I have tomorrow off."

"Sounds good." Alicia rose to her feet. "I have to go. It's late."

Blake stood up too. "Let me drop you off."

Alicia imagined how her tear-stricken face and swollen eyes would go down with the folks on the bus. No need to scare anyone tonight. "Okay."

"This is it," Alicia said as Blake parked his car in front of her house.

Blake looked up at the brownstone. "It's nice."

"Thanks. We are lucky to live here."

"We?" Blake gave her a questioning look.

"My roommates and I," Alicia replied. "Both Jasmine and Dana are residents at the hospital, but not in internal medicine. And they're also my friends."

"Okay. Maybe I'll get to meet them one of these days."

Alicia refused to think about what Blake meant. She'd had a good time working with him on the presentation, but everything would be over tomorrow, and they would go their separate ways. It had been fun while it lasted. "Anyway, thanks again for dropping me off."

Blake gave her a soft look. "I'll see you tomorrow in the auditorium," he said.

"Good night." Alicia opened the car door.

"Alicia ..." Blake touched her arm.

She turned towards him. Their eyes met. It was like time stood still. Alicia's heart pounded loudly in her ears, and she couldn't break his gaze. Blake leaned toward her, his eyes searching her face and then looking down at her lips.

Alicia's heart beat faster. She had to leave NOW or they would both regret what happened next. "Good night, Blake," she said, leaping out of the car and slamming the door. She ran up the front steps and refused to look back.

She was afraid she would change her mind.

CHAPTER 19

Blake smiled as Alicia hurried into the house. She was definitely intriguing —strong, funny, yet shy. He loved talking to her, and it felt like they had been friends forever. And yes, he had to face the truth—he was very attracted to her. But it was more than her beauty. There was something so special about her, like he would be making a big mistake if he didn't even give himself the chance to see if she was the one.

In the moment, he had wanted to kiss her. But it hadn't been the right time. Good thing she'd taken off when she did. That would have been moving too fast, and he wasn't yet sure if they were going to end up in a relationship. If he wanted them to be more than friends, then he had to do it right. He couldn't afford another failed relationship, and he was almost certain it would hurt way more than the last time if it didn't work out. So he had to give it his best shot.

His phone rang beside him. Blake picked it up from the console and looked at the screen. It was his father, Phillip Dexington. He put on his Bluetooth headset and clicked it.

"Hello, Dad."

"Blake. How is the presentation going?"

"We are all set for tomorrow."

"Listen. Plans have changed. Cunningham and his team have been able to convince the rest of the board to schedule an emergency meeting tomorrow morning to discuss the succession planning efforts. You know we had planned this presentation as the first opportunity to introduce you to the hospital leadership. They are highly intelligent people, and it was important we spoke to them in their own language. But now it has become much more than that. It is now going to be your primary introduction springboard to the board, and we need you to present alone so that it can be as effective as it needs to be. The board plans to attend the symposium in the morning before the emergency board meeting. We are going to take advantage of that."

Blake felt sucker-punched. This was bad news. "Dad, that wouldn't be fair. Alicia Montgomery and I are expected to present together. She's worked so hard on this, and it would be unjustifiable to cut her off."

"Blake, unfortunately, that is no longer an option. It's important that the board accepts you as my replacement as soon as possible, and they need to see what you are capable of. You know Cunningham has been whispering into the ears of the other board members that you are not qualified to be the CEO and Chairman after I retire. I've heard Harrison is the one behind him —he's still bitter after all these years that he didn't get Arthrodev, which has made us millions of dollars, despite how affordably we priced it to ensure the knee implants got into the hands of those who needed them most. Your refusal to present alone could turn the board against us."

Blake sighed. He knew he could not refuse his father. He had promised him he would do everything required of him to make the succession planning process as seamless as possible. He knew the transition wasn't easy for his father, but the mini-stroke he'd suffered had been a warning for him to start scaling things back, and his mother had insisted that Blake was ready.

"We've arranged the schedule so you'll be speaking first instead. The affected presenter has already been notified. This is confidential for now, as we don't want Cunningham and his team to get wind of what we've planned. Unfortunately, that means keeping it from Dr. Montgomery. I know you are upset, but it is what it is, son. I have to go. I can hear your mother calling my name. Good luck! I'm sure you'll do great." The line went dead.

Blake raked his hands through his hair and rested his head on the steering wheel. What was he going to do? There wasn't even enough time to come up with a solution. How was he going to face Alicia? From their conversation, he could infer that she needed the money for Willow's treatment. And the presentation was this strong because of her hard work. She might never speak to him again after all this.

He rubbed his temples. Tonight was going to be a very long night.

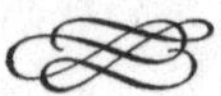

*A*licia got up and stepped away from the computer. She stretched her arms in front of her before letting them fall by her side. It was all done. The last patient had been taken care of.

Alicia had been at the wards since six a.m. seeing to her patients and reviewing the sign out from the night float team. She'd been given the morning off because of the presentation, but she had wanted to make sure that all her patients were seen. Another resident would be covering for her for the rest of the day, and the interns would be handling the rest. They would only ping her if there was an emergency they couldn't handle. But Alicia didn't expect that to happen; the other resident was more than capable.

The symposium was expected to start at nine a.m. Blake had assured her he would make sure the presentation was all set up, so Alicia wasn't worried. They were expected to present at noon. There was still enough time if she needed to crosscheck everything was in place.

Blake. She hadn't slept very much last night. She'd tossed and turned thinking about the almost kiss. One minute she was chiding herself for running away, the other she was glad she hadn't stayed. Regardless, she was looking forward to seeing him today.

As she got ready to leave the ward, a nurse ran up to her. "Dr. Montgomery, Mr. Mendoza just went into shock. We need you now." Mr. Mendoza was one of the new patients who had been admitted for acute pancreatitis. Alicia had a consult out to the hepatologists to see him during their round.

Alicia clicked out of the EMR system and raced to the patient's bedside. Ten minutes later, they had stabilized Mr. Mendoza. The liver team arrived just as Alicia finished, so she stayed on while they saw him and made the decision to take over his case.

She looked at her watch. It was now nine-forty-five a.m. The symposium must have started. She would update Mr. Mendoza's progress notes and then head over to the auditorium.

As she got to the central nursing station, she noticed the nurses stopped speaking once they saw her. What was that all about? Alicia chose to ignore them and worked on her updates at the computer terminal.

"Congratulations, Alicia."

Alicia looked up to see Liam Wang, a fellow second-year resident—whose features indicated he'd fought a war with pimples in his teenage years and lost— leaning against the station counter.

"For what?"

"For the presentation. But I was surprised to see Blake presenting alone. I'd heard you two were speaking together."

Alicia straightened. She didn't think she'd heard right. "What are you talking about?" She could sense the nurses had stilled and were eavesdropping on the conversation.

Liam raised an eyebrow. "Don't tell me you didn't know. Blake finished his presentation about twenty minutes ago. The auditorium has been buzzing with how good he was."

Alicia stiffened. She couldn't believe her ears. Blake had presented, and without her knowledge? Impossible! That would only mean one thing—she had been betrayed. That was out of the question. Not from the man that had almost kissed her last night. Why would Blake betray her? But the only way she could find out the truth was to see for herself.

Alicia's hands shook as she signed off from the computer terminal. She thanked Liam and hurried off in the direction of the auditorium.

She ignored the chatter that followed in her wake.

CHAPTER 21

*B*lake smiled as the board member shook his hand, but he wasn't really listening to what the man was saying. All he knew was that he needed to get to Alicia fast before anyone else did. He was afraid the news might have reached her ears by now, and he wanted to be there to explain what had happened.

Even though the presentation had been a success, that didn't take away the awful feeling he had in his stomach for the way everything had gone down. With the possibility of losing her before him, Blake realized that Alicia was more important to him than he had imagined.

The board meeting had taken place immediately after his presentation and hadn't lasted long. It had been a unanimous vote to have him take over from his father after he retired. They'd been satisfied with his qualifications and his keen insight into every aspect of the business—Blake had always worked in various sections of the family's conglomerate since his teenage years, so he knew the business in and out. He'd only stopped when he'd gone away for medical school and then residency, but had kept in touch with all the progress reports.

The handoff process would take about two years, during which time Blake would finish his residency. But he could now work side-by-side with his father in an official capacity until the transition was complete. His father would still maintain an advisory role even after retirement.

Blake had been on pins and needles since that morning, and not because of the presentation. He'd picked up his phone to call Alicia before the symposium began, but had remembered his father's warning and stuffed it back in his pocket. He wasn't even sure how he'd made it through the talk; he had probably spoken on autopilot. He'd tried her line once his session was done, but it had gone straight to voicemail. He had to find her now.

He thanked the board member and turned away from him.

That was when he saw her.

"That was a great presentation," an elderly man in an expensive suit said to Blake. He stood outside the nearest conference room to the auditorium, and Alicia saw him shake hands with the man.

"Thank you," she heard Blake say.

"I'll expect more from you in the future," the man replied. They shook hands again, and then Blake turned.

Their eyes met. And in that moment, Alicia saw the truth written clearly on his face.

He had betrayed her.

Alicia felt cold all over and staggered backwards. She'd been sure he wasn't like the other guys. How could Blake do this to her? She'd thought they'd become friends who truly respected each other. Was this who he really was?

"Alicia ..." Blake stepped tentatively towards her.

"How could you?" Alicia said. When Blake said nothing and didn't deny it, Alicia's heart twisted in pain, and she almost doubled over. She had been a fool and had fallen into his trap.

"Alicia ..." He reached out his hand.

"Don't touch me, Blake! I never should have trusted you." Alicia's body trembled. She had to get away. She turned and headed in the opposite direction.

"Alicia! Wait!" Blake called after her.

Alicia ignored him and ran blindly. Tears swelled behind her eyelids and threatened to spill over. She needed to find somewhere, anywhere to be alone.

"Alicia!" she heard again from behind her. But Alicia refused to stop. She needed to get as far away from him as possible.

Alicia saw the sign for the ladies' room up ahead on the left. She shoved the door open and ran into one of the open stalls and locked it behind her. There was no way he would follow her in here. She would stay here as long as she needed to make him go away.

Alicia sat on the closed toilet bowl and wrapped her arms around herself. She felt empty, dead on the inside. She'd taken a chance on Blake and allowed him to get close to her.

And he had betrayed her.

$\mathcal{A}$licia lost track of how long she stayed on the toilet seat. It turned out the bathroom was empty most of the time, except for the occasional foot traffic. It was a good place to hide if one wanted to be alone. And right now, she was the only person in it. The other stalls were empty.

She looked at her watch. It was three p.m. Goodness. She didn't know she had been in the bathroom for that long. Then she remembered what had brought her here, and she put her head on her knees. She had worked hard for this presentation, but it had been for nothing. Blake. She thought she generally had a good read on men. How had she not known he was a wolf in sheep's clothing?

Her heart ached as if a nail had been hammered into it. What Blake had done in cutting her out from the presentation had been a big deal. But if she was truthful to herself, it hurt more because she had begun to like him. Not as a colleague, but as a man. She had allowed herself to be vulnerable to him, and this was how he had paid her back, stomping all over her heart.

Alicia sighed. She could feel a headache coming on. Now, how was she going to pay for Willow's treatment? Since she didn't speak at the symposium, she might get five thousand dollars, but that wasn't even guaranteed given how everything had played out. Her trust in Blake had betrayed Willow, who was depending on her to come through for her. Willow, who didn't deserve any of this. Alicia had failed her yet again.

Tears gathered behind Alicia's eyelids. *You can't cry now, you don't deserve to cry*, she thought. She took a deep quivering breath.

Her phone rang. Alicia hesitated for a moment—she just wanted to be alone. But she pulled her phone from her coat pocket and looked at the screen. It was Dr. Hartwood. She pressed the answer button.

"Alicia, that was a great presentation!" the professor said. What a nice way to make Alicia feel worse. She rubbed her right temple. The headache seemed to have increased in intensity.

"Congratulations on winning the ten-thousand-dollar cash award! And I heard Blake made quite a case for you to the board," the professor continued.

"What?" Alicia sat up straight.

"Before he started the presentation, he stated that both of you had compiled the deck, and unfortunately, you couldn't present due to circumstances beyond your control. So when your team won the cash award, he insisted you also get the matching ten thousand dollars, which the symposium committee was more than happy to agree to, given how much wonderful feedback they'd gotten from the external guests." The professor chuckled. "That was quite some passionate speech he gave."

Alicia was thunderstruck. She didn't know what to say.

"I heard he even requested for additional

funding from the hospital board, to cover experimental cystic fibrosis treatment for pediatric patients who qualify for it," Dr. Hartwood continued. "The board passed the motion for the funding to be provided. Now, why do I think this is related to you for some reason?"

It dawned on Alicia what Blake had done, and she felt like a horrible human being. She'd judged him without listening to him.

"Thanks for telling me, Dr. Hartwood."

"Good work, Alicia. We hope to see more from you in the future." The professor ended the call.

Alicia jumped up from the toilet. One thing was certain—she had to find Blake immediately.

And it was amazing how the headache had suddenly disappeared.

Alicia hurried back to the auditorium. Her shoulders relaxed when she saw Blake talking to some other doctors outside its entrance, and she waited. The door to the auditorium was ajar, and only a few people remained inside. It seemed the symposium was over.

He soon finished chatting with them and looked up. His face went blank at the sight of her. Blake walked toward her. Alicia waited with bated breath, but when he reached her, he strode right past her.

She reached out and grabbed his arm. "Blake, please wait."

He stopped walking, but did not turn. "Not here," he said in a cold voice. He strode toward one of the smaller conference rooms. Alicia struggled to keep up with his long quick strides. He opened the door, and they stepped in. The room was empty. He turned and faced her, his eyes expressionless. "What is it, Dr. Montgomery?"

Crap. She must have really hurt him for him to call her that and not Alicia.

"Dr. Hartwood told me what happened. Blake, I should have waited to hear what you had to say."

Blake sighed and his shoulders relaxed a little. "You had every right to be mad. I'm sorry for not telling you ahead of time about the change in presentation. I got a call last night—after we parted ways—telling me about it, and that I had to keep the information secret, even from you."

"Thanks for going to bat for me for both the cash award and the funding for Willow."

"I wanted to make it up to you." Blake reached out his hand and brushed a strand of her hair away from her face. "Why do you have such an effect on me?"

Alicia's breath hitched. She didn't know what to say to that. It seemed the temperature in the room had just ratcheted up. His touch sent tingles racing from her head to her toes. Alicia swallowed.

But she couldn't afford to feel this way. The presentation was over, and there could be nothing between them. She tried to change the subject.

"I have to go see Willow."

Alicia could tell Blake noticed what she'd done, but he didn't press further.

"Can I come along?" he asked. "It would be great to meet her."

CHAPTER 24

Alicia called Dr. King on her way over to the pediatric unit and told him the good news. The doctor was ecstatic and promised to get Willow in the program right away. Alicia also left a voicemail for Carla about it.

"Hi, Willow." Alicia entered Willow's cubicle in the pediatric ward and stood next to her bed. The room was painted a soft pink color with cartoon characters and superheroes on different sections of the walls.

"Aunt Alicia!" Willow's grey eyes twinkled as she lifted her thin arms for a hug. She was dressed in a hospital gown; her short blond hair peeked out from a pink beanie hat decorated with petite bows and sparkling crystals.

"I see a new bow," she said, touching the purple and white polka dot mini bow. "It seems you have a new admirer," she teased Willow.

"You mean Paul? He's nice, but he's too quiet." Alicia couldn't imagine Willow around him. She was a chatterbox and could talk ten miles per second.

She sat on the bed, and Willow leaned against her. "How are you today, my little pumpkin?" Alicia asked softly, putting her arms around her.

Willow beamed up at her. "They turned off the oxygen. I can breathe without it." Alicia's heart squeezed with love at the sight. She grinned back.

"Wow, he is handsome," Willow said as she craned her neck beyond Alicia to see Blake. "Is that your boyfriend, Aunt Alicia?"

Alicia blushed pink. She had forgotten Blake was with her. "Willow, meet my colleague, Blake. Blake, meet Willow."

"Hi, Willow. So nice to meet you. Alicia, you didn't tell me I was coming to meet a princess," Blake responded.

Willow chuckled. "That's so cheesy." Then

her face turned serious. "I like you. Would you like to be my aunt's boyfriend?"

"Willow!" Alicia stared at her in horror.

"I would love to, if she would have me," Blake said.

Alicia's ears turned bright red. She wished the ground would open up now and swallow her. How could Blake say something like that even in jest? "Stop it, you two. You know what? I think I'm going to get some water." She grabbed the empty water jug from the night-stand. "I'll be right back." She didn't wait for either of them to answer and stepped out of the room. She heard a chuckle and a giggle as she left.

Alicia refilled the water jug from the dispenser in the small kitchenette on the same floor and headed back to Willow's room. She stopped at the door and watched what was going on in the room.

Willow was grinning at whatever Blake was telling her, and then she burst into laughter. The musical sound filled the whole room. It had been a while since Alicia had seen Willow laugh like that. Not since her sister died. The animated conversation between them unfurled something that had been lying dormant within her—a desire she couldn't put into words.

Blake turned to look at her at that moment. Warm butterflies fluttered in Alicia's stomach. The rest of the room seemed to fade away.

Alicia cleared her throat to shake away the effect on her. "I'm back," she said and walked to Willow's side. She placed the water jug back on the nightstand.

"Aunt Alicia, we were just talking about how you are scared of cockroaches," Willow responded with a mischievous grin.

"Willow!"

"Sorry." She had a rueful look on her face, but Alicia knew she wasn't repentant.

"We need to go." Alicia grabbed Blake's arm and pulled him up. "I'll come back later tonight, sweetheart." She gave Willow a kiss on the forehead.

"Bye, Blakey." Willow lifted her hands toward Blake. Blake gave her a quick hug.

"She's wonderful," Blake said. They were standing in the hallway outside of Willow's unit.

"Thanks for letting me meet her. If not, I wouldn't have known you are a scaredy cat around cockroaches."

Alicia jabbed Blake in the side.

"Ouch! What was that for?" Blake doubled over, clutching his side. Suddenly, he leaned forward. "Is that a cockroach?" he asked, pointing at a corner of the wall.

Alicia shrieked, grabbing his arm. Blake burst out laughing.

"Blake, how dare you?" She was not amused. Blake took off down the hallway, laughing as he went. Alicia ran after him and tackled him.

"I'm sorry, I'm sorry." A grin split his face as he tried to fend off Alicia's hands. A janitor pushing a cart along the hallway gave them a puzzled look.

"Let me make it up to you," Blake said. Alicia stopped and looked at him. "Let me take you out to celebrate."

"Isn't it a bit too early?" Alicia looked at her watch. "It's just a few minutes to four."

"I think it's fine, and you don't have to change."

Alicia looked down at what she was wearing. It was a navy blue pinstripe dress paired with low pumps. She did look nice.

"Come on, let's go." Blake grabbed her by the hand and led her to the elevators. Once they were in and the elevator doors had shut, he pulled his wallet from his pocket and swiped it against a card reader on the elevator control panel, which turned an indicator button on it from red to green. Then he pressed the button for the top floor.

"Where are we going?" Alicia asked.

"You'll see." They rode the elevator in silence until it stopped. The doors opened to reveal the rooftop. Alicia stepped out to see a helicopter on a helipad spinning its rotors with a pilot already seated in the cockpit.

She turned to Blake. "Are you serious?"

Blake grinned. "You'll love where we're going. Trust me." He led the way to the cabin and opened the door for Alicia to climb in. Once she was settled in, he closed the door and then walked over to the other side and boarded it as well.

The helicopter lifted off once they were all strapped into their seats. Alicia had taken a helicopter ride before, but it had been a long time and she had forgotten how much she'd enjoyed it the first time. And it was much better this time around with Blake seated next to her, his woody mint scent wrapping around her like a blanket. But did she really have a right to be here?

"Blake, should we be riding this? Isn't it the hospital's?" she said into the headset.

"No. It's mine."

Alicia stilled. Not even his father's, but his? She'd forgotten for a second that he was supposed to be rich, but it had never occurred to her that he might be richer than she'd imagined. Which meant he was way out of her league.

"I need you to stop thinking whatever you're thinking," Blake said into the headset.

"What am I thinking?"

"About how wealthy I am. I'm still Blake, your colleague and friend."

"So we are friends now?"

"Aren't we? I thought that boat sailed away long ago."

"Ha ha, very funny."

"We are almost there."

Alicia looked down and gasped. She recognized the views of the Charles River with its companions, Harvard and MIT, and the antique

Beacon Hill surrounded by a modern city. They were in Boston! "What are we doing here?"

Blake grinned. "You'll see."

Alicia pressed her face against the window till they landed on what looked like a private helipad. Once the rotors stopped spinning, Blake jumped down and then strode over to the other side to help Alicia down. The air was definitely nippy in Boston. "I thought I read there were no helipads in Boston apart from the airport," she said.

"There are no public access helipads, you mean. This one is private and belongs to a family friend who owns the building. One of the Boston hospitals has one for medical flights." Blake handed Alicia a fall jacket. "You can leave your medical coat in the helicopter."

Alicia removed her medical coat and handed it to Blake before donning the jacket. It fit perfectly. Blake put on a grey coat as well and dropped their medical coats in the cabin. He turned to the pilot and gave him a thumbs up. The pilot nodded. "Let's go," he said to Alicia.

He led her down the elevators and into a limousine with tinted windows parked on the curb. The ride felt luxurious, and Alicia enjoyed the warm leather seats. After a few minutes, the limousine stopped moving, and Blake got out and held out a hand to Alicia. "We are here."

Alicia took his hand and got out. Her hand rushed to cover her mouth.

"What do you think?" Blake said.

"I can't … seriously … We are at the Boston Symphony Hall?"

"Why don't we go in?" Blake held her by the hand and led her into the historical building.

The rest of the evening was more breathtaking than Alicia could have dreamed. They had a light dinner in one of the other halls overseen by one of the best chefs in Boston, and then they moved into the main symphony hall, which was breathtaking in its shoebox design. Blake and Alicia were the only guests in the concert hall, and the Boston Symphony Orchestra delighted Alicia with an all-Mozart program—the three-movement No. 34 in C major, Linz Symphony No. 36 in C major, and Symphony No. 40 in G minor.

The music was ethereal. From the sophisticated fanfare-like opening of No. 34—which moved through an unpredictable lyrical second theme and a suspenseful cadence, before closing out with a finale that evoked the sense of a fast-paced opera—to the mellowness of the No. 36, which began with slow movements of the trumpets and drums and ended with a danceable minuet. And finally, the orchestra played the No. 4 in G minor, which opened with violas and a soft piano, flashed with a fiery minuet, and ended with a finale that sought to close all wounds and bring the listener home. Each piece had a story that spoke to her heart.

By the end, Alicia had tears running down her cheeks and barely noticed when Blake put his arm around her and drew her in. It had been a moment of sharing and understanding pain and grief, and then choosing to hold tightly to hope and a dream for the future.

Alicia would never forget tonight. Blake had given her a wonderful gift that had healed her soul. They returned to Dexington shortly after, and Alicia stopped by the hospital to see Willow, and then moved on to the wards to see her patients. Blake offered to return to pick her up and drop her home, and Alicia asked him not to worry about it.

By the time Alicia got down to the hospital lobby, her ankles hurt from the pumps she'd worn. She'd forgotten it was hard to get cabs at this time. She wished she hadn't been so quick to turn Blake down. *If there's a next time, I won't hesitate to take him up on the offer*, she thought.

She limped to the hospital entrance and stepped outside. And then she couldn't believe her eyes. Blake was leaning against his red sports car and had changed into a pair of jeans and button-down shirt with rolled up sleeves. He looked delectable.

Hallelujah! Alicia couldn't help the smile that broke out on her face. It was like he'd read her mind and known what she'd need. For a moment, Alicia enjoyed the feeling of having someone waiting for her. But she then shelved the thought. This wasn't real. The best she could do was enjoy the moment while it lasted.

"I didn't know you would come back," Alicia said.

Blake straightened and stepped toward her. "I figured your feet would be aching by now, and it wasn't a big deal for me since I live close by," Blake replied.

Her heart sang. She liked this man who anticipated her needs before she thought about them. "Thank you," she said. He held the door open for her, and Alicia climbed in. He closed the door, and then moved to the driver's side and got in as well. Then they were driving away from the hospital.

The leather car seats were super comfortable, and the headrest cradled her head nicely. Before she knew it, Alicia had dozed off. She felt a hand on her arm, and she opened her eyes. They had arrived in front of her apartment. She'd slept all through the trip home!

"I'm sorry," she said as she scrambled to sit up. "I didn't know I was this tired. Thank you for bringing me home."

"No worries. I do have a favor to ask," Blake said. He tapped his fingers on the steering wheel.

"What is it? Hopefully, it's something I can help you with."

"Be my date for tomorrow's gala."

Alicia looked sharply at him. "You are kidding, right?"

"I'm serious."

"I'm not sure that's a good idea. I've never been to one before." Attending galas wasn't something that people in Alicia's circles did. And she couldn't afford to spend any money now on an expensive dress.

"It would be fun. You'll be saving me from boredom," Blake pleaded with Alicia with a twinkle in his eyes.

"I don't know. I don't have anything to wear."

"I can take care of that."

"That won't be right."

"If you come with me, I'll make you pancakes with smiley faces," Blake said.

He knew how to get her. Pancakes? Alicia was already salivating. Given what she knew now about his cooking, the pancakes would probably be delicious. And what harm could one gala do? "Homemade with chocolate syrup?" she asked.

"Yes."

"Deal. But I'll take care of the dress myself."

CHAPTER 25

Blake stepped into his apartment, padded over to his couch and slumped into it. It had been a long day and he was tired, but it had been worth it. He couldn't forget the look on Alicia's face as she'd listened to the symphonies. He'd made the arrangements while he brooded on what to do the night before the presentation. He was glad it had paid off. He could have stayed and studied her face all day. That was how much he was entranced by her.

He leaned back and closed his eyes. When he'd agreed to come back to Dexington, he'd never known his life would change this much. He had been all focused on helping his father and taking care of his patients. And then he'd met Alicia.

She was smart, funny, beautiful, and loved her patients. And best of all, she was single. He'd never thought he'd find someone he was willing to open his heart to. But Alicia had made it easy. And even though she appreciated money, she was fiercely independent and didn't really care about his wealth. The more he spent time with her, the more he liked what he saw. Not that she was perfect—neither was he, and perfection was overrated anyway. He'd sworn off women, but he found that he was willing to give a relationship another chance. Because of her.

Knowing that she was Willow's guardian didn't bother him. He loved children, and anyone could tell that Willow was special. He was the one that was lucky to know her. They'd hit it off, so he didn't see any problem there.

"Hey, Blake."

Blake opened his eyes. He'd thought he was alone in the apartment. "Josh, I didn't know you were here."

Josh yawned and ambled over to sit next to Blake. "I sent you a text that I was coming over.

Or were you too busy with Alicia to remember your best friend?" Blake saw a grin split Josh's face.

"What's going on, man?" Blake asked.

"I'm good. I can see you are in a great mood. I'm going to sit over here and watch some soccer before going back to the hospital."

"Are you on-call?"

"Sort of."

"What do you mean sort of? You are or you aren't."

"It's a secret. Just like the one you are keeping about Alicia."

"I think you need some thrashing on the court. It's been a while. Maybe your mouth will stay shut once we are done."

"Okay, okay, I'll pass for now." Josh yawned again. "Let me enjoy this downtime in peace." An instrumental ringtone split the air. Josh looked at Blake. "Is it Alicia?" Blake threw a pillow at Josh's head. "Ouch! That hurts."

Blake pulled his phone from his pocket. It was his grandmother, Helen Dexington, his favorite person in the world.

"Hi, Grandma!"

His grandmother chuckled from the other

end of the line. "How are you doing, my little puppy smushy you?"

Blake laughed. "Grandma, I'm no longer five."

"Exactly," his grandmother said.

Blake chuckled. Sometimes he didn't know what to make of her.

"So who is she?" she asked.

"Grandma, I don't know what you're talking about."

"Honey, you think because I'm in Europe I don't know what's going on? Spill it." She giggled. "Alex, slow down."

"Grandma, what are you doing with Grandpa? Wait, I don't want to know. Forget I asked."

"What? My dear, this is what you should pray for. That at this age, your partner and best friend still finds you desirable. Alex, stop." She giggled again. "I gotta go, dear. I'm busy. We'll talk later."

"Bye, Grandma." Blake ended the call and leaned back on the couch with a disbelieving shake of his head.

"What is it, Blake?" Josh asked.

"I'm not sure. I think Grandma and Grandpa are about to get it on."

Josh laughed. "You should see your face. Go, Grandpa."

Blake scrubbed his face with his hands. "It's going to take me a while to unsee this."

Josh roared with laughter.

licia sighed. "What did I get myself into?" Most of her clothes were strewn on her bed and spilling over onto the floor.

Dana poked her head into Alicia's room through the slightly open door. "What's the matter?"

Alicia exhaled. "I need a dress for this evening's gala. I can't find anything in my wardrobe that works." She gestured at the clothes.

Alicia heard a sound and looked up to see Jasmine's head above Dana's.

"Did you say gala?" Jasmine asked.

"Yes, Blake invited me to the Bone Marrow Awareness Gala," Alicia said.

"Ooh!" Jasmine and Dana responded in unison.

"You guys are not helping! Really, what am I going to wear?" Alicia plopped down despondently on the bed.

"I think I have just the dress for you. Hold on." Jasmine disappeared for two minutes and then reappeared with a garment bag in her hands. She entered Alicia's room and placed it on the bed. She zipped down the bag to reveal a gorgeous ivory gown with a crisscross bodice that flowed through a cinched waist into chiffon panels.

Alicia's eye widened, and she touched the edge of the dress as if afraid she might stain it. "This is beautiful," she said in a whisper.

"Come on. Try it on. No time like the present," Jasmine said.

Alicia donned the dress. It was so easy to wear, and it hugged what curves she had in the right places. She felt like a princess as it flowed beautifully around her.

"Oh my! You look stunning." Dana gawked at her in appreciation.

"Blake is going to have a heart attack," Jasmine agreed.

"Are you sure I can wear this?" Alicia asked Jasmine.

"Believe me, you'll be doing me a favor," Jasmine responded. "I think your gold strappy heels would be perfect with it. Then all you need is a little accent jewelry."

"I think I have just the piece to use. It was a graduation gift from my sister." Alicia reached into her wardrobe and pulled out a jewelry box. She opened it and looked at the gold earrings with their matching cuff.

She had found the box among her sister's things after her death. Willow had said it was supposed to be her graduation gift from medical school, and that her sister had been so excited when she'd brought it home. Alicia had found her name inscribed on the inside of the cuff. She had worn it once on the day she graduated but never again since then. But today would be a perfect day for it; she knew her sister would be proud of her if she was here.

Alicia lifted the pieces one by one and put them on.

"Perfect!" Dana said.

Alicia's phone beeped. She picked it up and

looked at the screen. It was a text message from Blake, saying he would be there in two hours.

"Shoot! He'll be here in two hours. I have to hurry." Alicia pulled off the dress as carefully as she could.

"Relax, relax. Take deep breaths, my friend. You have two hours," Dana told her.

Alicia took a deep breath. "Okay, I can do this." She smiled at Jasmine. "Thanks again."

"You're welcome," Jasmine replied. "Have fun tonight!" She took Dana's hand. "Come on." Jasmine left the room and dragged Dana away with her.

An hour and fifty-five minutes later, Alicia was ready. "How do I look?" she asked as she stepped down the stairs. She had done up her hair in a Grecian style instead of her usual ponytail.

"Oh, wow!" Dana exclaimed from the couch, looking up from the magazine she was reading.

"You look adorable! I think that dress was made for you," Jasmine said. The doorbell rang.

"I'll get it." Jasmine raced to the door and opened it. "Hi Blake, please come in."

"Hi, you must be Alicia's roommate," Blake responded with a smile and stepped into the living room.

"Yes, I'm Jasmine, and that's Dana over there." Jasmine motioned towards the couch.

"Hi!" Dana said.

"Hello! Nice to meet you both," Blake said.

"Hi, Blake," Alicia said.

Blake turned at her voice and froze. He looked at her from head to toe in appreciation. "Wow! You look ... stunning!" He couldn't stop staring at her.

"You clean up real nice too," Alicia said. Blake wore a black two-tone custom tuxedo with matching bow tie and custom leather shoes.

They stared at each other for a few moments.

"Ahem," Jasmine cleared her throat. "We're still here. Hello!"

Alicia felt heat creep up her face. "I think we should get going," Alicia said to Blake.

Blake turned to Dana and Jasmine. "Ladies, it was a pleasure meeting you. I hope to see you around some other time. Have a good evening." Jasmine smiled back, and Dana giggled.

Blake held out his arm to Alicia, and she looped hers with his. They stepped out of the house and down the front steps. Blake walked Alicia to the car and opened the passenger door for her.

"Thank you," Alicia said as she slid in.

Blake walked around to the driver's side, entered the car, and started the engine. He turned to Alicia. "You look really beautiful," he said.

"Are you saying I've never looked beautiful?" Alicia teased him.

"Fishing for compliments, are we? You know you've always been a head turner."

Alicia felt the heat all the way to her toes. This man would be her undoing if she wasn't careful. She looked away from him to stare ahead. A hint of a smile hovered at the corners of her lips. "Let's go. We are going to be late."

CHAPTER 27

Blake and Alicia arrived at the gala. It was being held at the Russellmore Hotel, an old historic hotel in downtown Dexington. Alicia had to hold back from gawking as they entered the ballroom. It was like all the wealth and beauty of Dexington were gathered in one place.

Massive crystal chandeliers hung from a high dramatic ceiling, women in various shades of stunning gowns complemented by sparkling jewelry mingled with men in smart tuxedos, and waiters in white jackets holding trays laden with hors d'oeuvres or champagne flutes moved among them. Alicia could see what looked like a balcony beyond a set of doors on the right.

Everything looked so lovely, but Alicia felt a bit out of place. This was not a world that she was used to.

Heads turned as they walked into the room. Blake nodded at a few folks and shook hands with others. It was obvious he was a natural in this kind of setting. He introduced Alicia to everyone as he went, and she gave the appropriate smiles and nods in return, but their faces and matching names were a blur for her. It was a bit too much to take in.

Someone called Blake's name. Blake turned to see who it was and then whispered in Alicia's ear. "I'll be right back." He strode across the room to greet the elderly couple who had beckoned him over.

Alicia didn't know what to do next. She grabbed a glass of wine from a passing waiter and nursed the drink. She didn't see any familiar faces so she wandered towards a corner of the room and watched the activity from there.

"Look who the cat dragged in," a voice behind her said.

Alicia turned to see Mandy—one of her former classmates from Harvard—draped in a glittering wine gown, her blond curls in a loose chignon. Mandy and Alicia had never gotten along since their first year. She'd had a thing against Alicia, though Alicia had never been able to figure out why. Mandy had never passed up any opportunity to taunt or dig at her. Alicia had breathed a sigh of relief when they'd graduated and Mandy had stayed back in Boston for residency while Alicia had moved to Dexington. So to say she wasn't happy to see Mandy was an understatement.

"I wonder how you got in," Mandy said with an ugly curve of her mouth. "This place is not for church rats."

Alicia felt her face heat up. But the comment was not worthy of a response. Today was a happy day, and she planned to have it stay that way. She looked around for Blake but didn't see him. She ignored Mandy and tried to move away to another section of the room. But one minute she was upright, and the next she had faltered and her wine had tipped over and spilled on her dress.

"Oops. Sorry!" Mandy said with a grin on her face. Mandy had tripped her. She looked up to see people giving her curious glances from across the room. Others stared and whispered.

Alicia felt naked as if on display. She looked down at her dress and saw a spreading red patch from where the wine had spilled. The beautiful dress was ruined.

Alicia's blood boiled. Who did Mandy think she was? Fine, Alicia didn't belong here, but Dexington was her home turf, and Mandy had no right to disrespect her here. She resisted the urge to rush out of the room and instead pulled herself to her full height, smiled, and leaned toward Mandy. "I feel sorry for you," she said in a whisper. "I didn't know you were this insecure."

Mandy stuttered and turned beet red, matching her gown perfectly.

Alicia straightened and walked with her head held high toward the doors that led to the balcony, and avoided making eye contact with anyone. She was afraid that if she did, the trembling on her inside might erupt like a volcano.

As she got closer to the doors, Alicia felt a hand touch her arm, and she started. She turned to see Blake.

"That was a coup d'état," Blake whispered near her ear.

"Please take me out of here." Alicia couldn't keep the tremor from her voice.

Blake took one look at her face and moved to usher her through the balcony doors.

"My God, it is really you, Alicia," a voice said from behind her.

A coldness struck Alicia's core at the sound of the voice, and she shook. Her heart raced into a gallop. No way. It couldn't be.

She turned around and came face-to-face with the worst nightmare of her life.

CHAPTER 28

Alicia turned to see Charles heading toward her. She couldn't believe her eyes. It was him, the same Charles who had abandoned her many years ago, albeit a much older version of the lean blue-eyed blond teenager that she'd been in love with, dressed in a grey tuxedo with a black lapel. He sported an incredulous look on his face like he had seen a ghost.

Alicia's world collapsed, and her legs weakened. What was he doing here? She gripped Blake's arm so tight that she probably left marks on it.

Blake must have sensed something was

wrong because he rushed her onto the balcony and slammed the doors shut behind them.

Alicia stood trembling like a leaf. She couldn't believe she was seeing Charles here of all places.

Blake wrapped his arms around her. "It's okay," he said over and over again as he held her close and rubbed his hand up and down her left arm.

But it wasn't okay. Blake didn't know the truth. Maybe he would leave her once he found out. But she was already tired of carrying this secret, and she needed to let it out. She could tell Blake liked her—a lot. It was better if he found out now to give him a chance to leave before he burrowed too far into her heart.

Blake continued to hold her, and Alicia felt her heart rate returning to normal at the sound of his voice. The warmth from his arms around her calmed her. She nestled in a little further, and they stayed that way for a few minutes.

Blake leaned back and searched her face. "Can you tell me what happened?" he asked.

Alicia hesitated for a moment. This could change everything. But he deserved to know the truth. She took a deep breath and mustered up her courage. "That's Charles, Willow's father," she said.

"Willow's father?" She could see the confusion on Blake's face.

"Yes."

"But, that doesn't make sense. I thought Kevin, your sister's husband, was her father."

"Willow was adopted."

"But how do you know he is Willow's real dad?"

She stepped out of Blake's arms and looked out beyond the balcony. Little stars twinkled in the darkened sky, but she didn't really see them.

Only her mother and her sister had known. Alicia had never told anyone else. But it was time. She wrapped her arms around herself. "Because I'm Willow's birth mom," she said.

CHAPTER 29

"Alicia," Blake called her in a softened tone.

Alicia was afraid to turn around. What if he hated her? She wouldn't blame him—she hated herself too. But she wasn't ready to face the condemnation she was sure to find in his eyes.

Blake placed his hands on her shoulders and turned her to face him. "Alicia, look at me."

Alicia lifted her eyes to look into his. She expected anything else but what she saw in his eyes—there was only empathy.

"Tell me," he said softly and pulled her closer.

The story spilled out. She and Charles had grown up next to each other. Alicia had lived with her mom—her father had passed away when she was still in elementary school. Charles had been her next-door neighbor and childhood friend for many years. They had played and gone to school together, ridden bikes together, and even their mothers had been friends.

Then one summer, when they were fifteen, everything changed. Alicia grew from the gangly girl with pig tails into a beautiful young lady, and Charles changed as well. Her feelings for Charles grew into something stronger, and she saw it mirrored in his eyes. They talked about their dreams for the future and how they wanted to go to the same schools. She thought they were in love, and one night after Charles climbed into her room, Alicia was overwhelmed with emotion and gave herself to him. After that day, she became afraid that things could go wrong and decided it was best if they abstained from further sex.

Two months and a bucketload of early morning sickness later, Alicia's mom found out she was pregnant. Alicia hadn't known that all it took was one time to get pregnant. After a lot of questions, she finally revealed to her mom that Charles was the father of the baby.

Alicia's mom called Charles' parents, who were out of town, to tell them what had happened. They told her they would be back home the next day and agreed to meet after work on their return to discuss it. The next morning, Alicia noticed Charles didn't show up for class. She came home after school to see a large moving truck in front of Charles' house. By the time Alicia's mom came home from work, Charles' house stood empty.

Alicia was devastated. Charles had abandoned her. She spiraled into a state of depression and couldn't eat or sleep and spent the next few days crying in dejection. Her mom, fearing for her health, called Alicia's elder sister, Mary, who had married and moved to Boston. Alicia had been a late child, so they were twelve years apart in age. Mary flew in and picked her up. But no matter what Mary did to help, Alicia couldn't seem to break free from the depression and the next seven months flew by in a haze. She ended up giving birth to a baby girl. The doctors later said she had postpartum depression.

"I was out of it the whole pregnancy," Alicia said. "And when Willow was born, I couldn't touch her even though I sat very close to her. It was like I was there, but not there at the same time. I knew she was mine and I wanted her—I would sit very close to her and stare at her all day—but somehow I didn't have the strength or courage to pick her up. In my head, I knew what I had to do to take care of her, but I couldn't get myself to do it."

She rubbed her eyes. "But then I wondered: how would the town treat her when they found out she was mine? Willow didn't deserve that kind of treatment. It was like if I touched her I would seal her fate. But I also knew I didn't deserve her. I felt unworthy of her, yet I didn't want to give her up.

"Fortunately, my mom had a sense of what was going on in my mind and asked my sister if she could foster her. I was so depressed that I could barely function, let alone take care of someone else. My sister was the one person I adored, and my mom knew I could let go even if only in the short term if Mary was the one who took care of Willow. You see, my sister had been trying for a long time to get pregnant and when Willow came, she poured all her love on her.

"By the time I got better, Willow had truly

blossomed in my sister's care, and I thought it would be selfish of me to try and get her back. I saw how much Mary, Kevin, and Willow had bonded as a family, and I knew taking Willow away would break their hearts."

Alicia let out an exhale. "On the other hand, I had no idea how I would raise her. My mother became sick after the incident, so I couldn't depend on her support. I knew going back to school was the best thing for me and Willow if I wanted to give her a good future. And I didn't want her tainted by my shame. She deserved to be the best she could be, and my sister provided that. So I gave my consent for my sister to adopt Willow, and I moved back home to finish school and take care of my mom.

"By stepping up to adopt Willow, my sister saved three lives—my life, Willow's, and her own. But the whole experience must have broken my mother's heart, because she had a heart attack a year later and died."

Alicia rubbed the back of her neck. "Willow was always sick in the beginning. When she was diagnosed with cystic fibrosis, I knew it was all my fault. If I hadn't met up with Charles, maybe she could have been born without the disease.

The doctors needed to run some tests for the biological father, so I tried calling Charles' number, but it had changed. A friend of my mother's somehow got their new address, and I sent them a letter with the request from the hospital. Two days later, I got a voicemail from Charles on our home phone, warning me to never reach out to them again. If not, he would spread the news throughout my town that I was the class whore. I've never seen or heard from him and his family since that day," Alicia finished.

Blake swore under his breath and wrapped his arms tighter around Alicia. In that moment, Alicia knew that everything would be okay. It didn't matter how things ended up between Blake and her—she had found a true friend in him.

Her heart felt light like she had just let go of a heavy load. She laid her head against Blake's shoulder. It felt good to be in his arms.

"Alicia, thank you for trusting me enough to tell me," Blake said. "I want you to know you did the best for Willow given the circumstances." Tears welled up behind Alicia's eyelids. "Hey, don't cry on me now." He wiped away a tear that trickled down Alicia's face. "You are strong and beautiful. Never doubt that. And I've seen how much you love Willow."

He swept a tendril of her hair away from her face. "But there's one more thing I think you need to do—you need to show this Charles guy that he has no power over you, and that he missed out when he let you go. That you've done nothing wrong, and you have no reason to run from him. Come on." Blake held out his hand to her.

Alicia wasn't sure what Blake had in mind, but she was willing to go with him. He opened one of the balcony doors and led her to the center of the ballroom. He motioned to the musicians, and they changed the song to a beautiful waltz.

"Blake, I don't know how to dance," Alicia protested. She tried to pull her hand away.

"Trust me and follow my lead. You'll be fine." Blake wrapped his arm around Alicia's waist and pulled her close.

It was like they were made for each other. After a few initial missteps, Alicia found herself floating in Blake's arms and moving in oneness with him. She became so caught up in the dance that his movements became hers as he led her around the ballroom, his eyes never leaving hers. The rest of the room faded away, and it was like there was no one else there except the two of them. They could dance this way forever if they wanted.

Once the music ended, the sound of clapping brought Alicia back to the present. She looked around to see the rest of the room applauding them. Her ears turned pink.

The music started again, and someone touched Blake's shoulder. Alicia saw it was Charles. "I believe it's my turn to dance with her," he said as he stood next to Blake and reached for Alicia's hand.

Blake looked at Alicia. Alicia nodded her head and Blake stepped away.

The next dance was a little different—Alicia overheard someone mention it was the foxtrot. Charles tried to dance with Alicia, but she just stood there with her arms folded.

"You don't want to dance?" he asked. "You are not that special you know." He leaned forward. "And I've already had you once," he whispered.

For the first time, Alicia was grateful that

Charles had run away from her life. The person standing right in front of her was who he really was. She leaned forward and whispered, "I don't want to ever see you around me again." Then she lifted her right high heel and stomped hard on his foot.

Charles hollered and clutched his foot, and as Alicia walked away, she heard a crash. She turned back to see food dumped all over Charles' tuxedo. It appeared he had bumped into a waiter that was walking by.

Alicia stifled a giggle and turned back to where Blake stood.

He was silently clapping for her.

Her heart flipped over.

CHAPTER 30

*B*lake couldn't have been prouder of Alicia than at that moment. She was a strong woman and a gem as far as he was concerned. What she'd gone through didn't change his perception of her. As a doctor, he'd seen how terrible pre- or post-partum depression could be, yet she had put Willow's needs above hers in the midst of it.

But he still felt like wringing Charles' neck for what he had put Alicia through. He'd never seen Charles before. Blake knew all the movers and shakers of Dexington society, and Charles wasn't one of them. He wondered who had invited him to the gala.

He saw Charles move toward the double doors that lead to the restrooms.

"Can you give me a minute?" he said to Alicia when she reached him. "I'll be back in a second."

Blake strode through the ballroom and the double doors. He entered the men's restroom and saw Charles using the urinal. Blake strolled past him and washed his hands in the sink at the far end. As he walked back to exit the restroom, he bumped hard into Charles.

"What the …?" Charles stuttered and jumped back as he splashed urine all over his feet and pants. He turned to see who had hit him from behind, but Blake was long gone.

Blake grinned as he sauntered back through the ballroom. *Jerk.* He soon reached Alicia. "Are you ready to leave?" he asked.

Alicia smiled at him, her eyelids drooping a little. "Yes, I am. I think I've had enough for one night," she said.

Blake held out his arm, and Alicia linked hers with his. As they reached the main hotel entrance, Blake called the attention of the head of security and whispered an instruction into his ear. The valet brought his car around, and Blake was helping Alicia into it when he saw security escorting Charles out. Charles was practically foaming at the mouth in protest.

Alicia was silent on the drive home. Blake said nothing, knowing she needed the space. He parked his car in front of her house and waited for her to speak.

"I'm glad I faced Charles," she said finally.

Blake placed his hand over Alicia's and squeezed it. "You did great," he said. Then he continued rubbing his thumb on her hand. That seemed to relax her.

Then their eyes met. There was electricity in the air between them, and Blake couldn't look away. He felt a magnetic pull towards Alicia, and he leaned in, his eyes searching hers for a reaction. She tilted her face toward him and closed her eyes. His fingers brushed her cheek, and he heard her sharp intake of breath. He leaned in more to kiss her lips.

His phone rang. Blake groaned inwardly. *Wrong timing.* He wanted to ignore the call, but the caller was persistent. He let out a sigh as he pulled back and picked up the phone. He pressed the answer button. "Hello, Dad." By now, Alicia had opened her eyes and was busy looking at her hands.

"Blake, I need you to come home. Please bring the girl along with you."

Blake lifted an eyebrow. How did his father know these things? He hadn't even been at the gala which was still going strong. "Which girl? Alicia?" he asked.

He saw Alicia's head whip up at the mention of her name.

$\mathcal{B}$lake drove Alicia to a massive stately mansion surrounded by a beautiful garden. Its enormous wrought iron gates opened of their own accord, and then they were driving up a circular driveway to the front of the home. Alicia admired the fountain at the center of the driveway. Soon they reached the top of the driveway, and Alicia noticed a man who looked to be middle-aged—though she couldn't really tell his age—in a crisp suit and bow-tie waiting near the entrance to the house.

"Who is that?" Alicia asked.

"That's Geoffrey. He has been our family butler since my dad was a kid. We consider him a member of our family. He's retired now and lives with his wife in a cottage at the back, but he still likes to work every now and then."

Blake parked the car at the end of the driveway, and they both stepped out.

"Welcome, Master Blake," Geoffrey said. He nodded at Alicia. "Miss."

"Thanks, Geoffery," Blake said. "How is the back doing? Hope it isn't acting up again."

"I'm doing quite well. The back is stronger than ever," Geoffrey replied. "Your parents are waiting in the living room."

"Geoffrey, why do I have this weird feeling you not only know why they've called me, but may have been involved in some way?"

The corners of Geoffrey's lips lifted in a smile. "I don't know what you're talking about."

Alicia stood there enjoying the easy banter between them.

"Really? I'm going to find out, Geoffrey," Blake said.

"Stop milling about and go on. Shoo!"

Blake laughed and grabbed Alicia's hand and propelled her toward the house. Alicia tried to slow her pace, but Blake held her hand fast, as if he knew that she wanted to bolt.

They passed through large French doors into

a cavernous foyer that led into a living room that was about five times the size of her somewhat large bedroom. Alicia couldn't believe her eyes. It was stunning, with multiple French doors that seemed to lead off to new areas of the house and a large winding central staircase that was the grandest feature of the room.

A distinguished-looking couple sat on a large cream sofa. Alicia assumed they were Blake's parents—it was obvious Blake took after the man's looks, even though the man had salt and pepper hair. The lady, on the other hand, had a pixie-cut that accentuated her beautiful blue-grey eyes. Blake stopped a few feet from where they sat. His parents stood. "Alicia, meet my parents, Phillip and Sarah Dexington. Mom, Dad, this is Alicia."

Phillip's piercing brown eyes assessed Alicia, which made her swallow. It was obvious Phillip was used to being in charge in any situation. He stretched out his hand and gave Alicia a firm handshake.

Sarah, on the other hand, gave Alicia a hug. Alicia liked her immediately. "You are the first girl that Blake has brought to the house," Sarah said with a smile.

Alicia gave Blake a sidelong glance, but he said nothing.

Phillip motioned to them to sit down. Alicia perched on an opposite couch. "I heard you asked Sam to kick someone out of the gala," Phillip said to Blake.

"Yes, I did. He did something offensive." Seeing the confusion on Alicia's face, Blake whispered into her ear, "Sam is the head of security at the gala."

Philip looked at Alicia. 'Was it because of Alicia?" he asked Blake. Blake didn't respond.

Alicia's thoughts froze. What were they talking about? Her eyes flipped from Phillip to Blake and back.

Phillip sighed. "That guy in question was Cunningham's guest. I'm sure he won't be happy, but I guess nothing can be done of it."

Alicia nudged Blake. "Who is Cunningham?" she whispered.

"A member of the hospital board," Blake whispered back.

"So, young lady ..." Philip addressed Alicia. "Alicia, right?"

"Yes, Alicia Montgomery, sir."

Phillip's eyebrows rose. "The one from the Bone Marrow presentation?"

"Yes, sir."

"So, Alicia, what's your relationship with my son?"

Alicia's mouth went dry. This wasn't supposed to be meet-the-parents day. "He is just …" she began.

"She is my girlfriend," Blake interjected.

Alicia gave Blake a dazed look and then turned back to Phillip. "We are just friends, sir," she corrected.

"Friends, you say?" Phillip said. She could tell he didn't believe her.

At this point, Sarah, who had been silent all along, cut in. She put a hand on Phillip's arm. "Oh, it's late, dear. Let the kids go back to whatever it is they were doing." She gave them a wink. Then she turned to Alicia and smiled. "It's great to meet you. You should visit us again sometime." To Blake, "Make sure she gets home okay."

"Yes ma'am" he said.

Sarah stood. Blake and Alicia did the same. Sarah hugged Alicia. "I heard you gave him a nice stomp. Good for you," she whispered, with Alicia still in her arms.

Alicia was speechless. Her face grew warm.

Sarah released her. "Alright you two. Off you go." She waved them away.

Once they were back on their way to Alicia's house, Alicia turned to Blake. "Your parents were not what I expected. They were nice, even your dad."

"Yes, I know they are great," Blake answered without taking his eyes off the road. "My mom seems to like you. She's the one that rules the house. If she likes you, you are all set."

"So Blake," Alicia folded her arms across her chest, "since when did I become your girlfriend?"

Blake took a quick look at Alicia. "It just kind of popped out. Did that bother you?"

"I would have preferred to be asked." Alicia twiddled her thumbs together.

"Alicia, would you like to be my girlfriend?"

"I don't think that's a good idea."

By this time, Blake had reached Alicia's

house. He pulled the car to a stop and turned to face her. "Why?"

"Isn't it obvious? I'm not really into the whole boyfriend-girlfriend thing. I just want to focus on becoming a doctor and taking care of Willow."

"Can't you do all three? I like you, Alicia. A lot."

Alicia sighed. "Couldn't we just be friends?"

Blake smiled at her. "I think you know we've passed the friends stage. We both know things about each other that others don't know. I like you, and I think you like me too."

Alicia frowned at Blake. "Who said I liked you?"

Blake leaned across the center console towards Alicia. Alicia's heart started beating faster. "You don't like me?" He moved a stray tendril away from her face.

Blake, stop! she wanted to say, but her mouth refused to move.

"Are you sure you don't like me?" He angled closer for a kiss. Alicia's heart galloped. "Say you don't like me."

Alicia bit her lip. "I ..."

Blake leaned away from her.

Wait! Why did you stop? she wanted to say.

"See? You can't deny that there's something going on between us," Blake said. He ran his right hand through his hair. "How about this? We'll just take it slow. I'm having a cookout next Saturday afternoon at my place with some friends. I would love for you to come, meet my friends, and generally get to know me better. Fair enough?"

"Okay, I'll be there. But I'm not your girlfriend."

"Yet." Blake got out and walked around to open the door for Alicia. Alicia stepped out. "Good night, my friend-that-is-not-yet-my-girlfriend." Blake shut the passenger door and reentered the car. He waited for her to climb up the front steps.

Then he gave her a quick wave and drove away.

Alicia took a shower and changed into a large T-shirt and shorts. She sat cross-legged on her bed and leaned against the headboard. Jasmine and Dana had pumped her for news about the gala until she was too tired to utter another word and begged off to go to bed.

She'd apologized to Jasmine about the dress and then told them the truth about Willow. Jasmine had assured her the dress didn't matter and given her a big hug, but Dana had been a bit aloof.

That's strange, she'd thought. She would ask Dana about it some other day.

Alicia leaned forward and stretched her arms in front of her on the bed. Her muscles no longer ached as much as they had before the shower. Awesome.

Her mind went back to all that had happened tonight. She'd been shocked at Blake's reaction—he had accepted everything she'd told him and hadn't judged her. Just like that. And it had been a night of firsts—attending the gala, meeting Blake's parents, and hearing Blake tell her that he liked her.

Blake's girlfriend. Warm butterflies fluttered in her stomach. She liked the sound of it. But did Blake really understand its ramifications? Accepting her meant he would have to accept Willow too. And there were implications for that down the road, especially since Alicia didn't date just for the sake of dating.

And would it really work? What if Blake regretted it the next day? *Aargh*. Alicia picked up her pillow and smashed her face into it. This was why she didn't do relationships. They were way too complicated.

She took a deep breath. *Maybe I'll just go to the cookout,* she thought. Even as friends, there was nothing wrong with meeting his other friends. *It wouldn't really mean anything, right?* she convinced herself.

She had nothing to lose.

CHAPTER 32

The next few days flew by. Alicia was back on night float duty, so both her days and nights were busy with admitting, attending to, and discharging patients. She also spent quite a significant amount of time teaching and guiding the medical student assigned to her team.

There was no time to really chat with Blake. He had his hands full taking on management responsibility for the hospital's strategy team, in addition to fulfilling his duties as a resident. Alicia wondered if he slept at all.

Saturday dawned bright and sunny with no hint of rain. November was a strange month in Dexington. Alicia would have expected the trees to have lost all their leaves by now—that was yet to happen. Not that she minded the weather, seeing that she wasn't really a big fan of snow.

Alicia slept in till ten a.m. Then she showered and headed over to Blake's apartment. The cookout was supposed to begin at eleven a.m.

"You made it!" Blake said as he let Alicia in and gave her a hug. "You look nice," he said. Alicia was wearing a pink T-shirt with white lettering that said "Doctors are not morons" paired with blue jean shorts and silver flats.

The corners of Alicia's mouth twitched in a smile. She had taken extra care in getting ready today and was pleased Blake had noticed. "You look good too," she said. Blake had on a white polo over tan Bermuda shorts.

Blake led Alicia through the double doors to the terrace. A barbecue station occupied one section of the terrace, a large game table occupied another, while lounging chairs surrounded a private pool that was centered in the space. Alicia could recognize some of the folks there—she'd seen them around the hospital—but most were unknown.

Blake led her around the space and introduced

his friends. Some looked at her with curiosity, others gave her welcoming smiles. Alicia was glad to see a familiar face, Josh, among them. Blake then led her to one of the reclining chairs.

"Sit. Let me grab you a drink. What would you like?" Blake asked.

"Do you have ginger ale?"

Blake lifted an eyebrow at Alicia. "I wouldn't have pegged you as a ginger ale kinda of gal. Maybe root beer."

"Ugh, I hate that stuff!"

"Really? I love it! Hold on one second while I grab your drink."

Blake headed to the wall next to the barbecue station and pressed a button on it. A cooling shelf slid open from the wall and he pulled a can of ginger ale from it. *Impressive.* He walked back and handed it to Alicia.

"Thanks," she said.

The doorbell chimed.

"I'll get it," Josh said. He strolled back into the apartment and came back a few minutes later with one of the most gorgeous young ladies Alicia had ever seen. She wore a short frock with sandals, a combination that looked expensive and perfect on her and complemented her blond curls.

Alicia noticed Blake's friends at the barbecue station exchange glances and then look at her. There was an awkwardness in the air, but Alicia couldn't pinpoint why. But from the cheerful way they greeted the young lady, it was clear that everyone knew who she was. The lady's face lit up as soon as she saw Blake, and she gave him a hug.

Alicia felt a stab of jealousy pierce her. Who was this lady, and why was she hugging Blake?

Blake returned her hug and then turned her towards Alicia. "Alicia, meet Laura, my friend."

Friend?

"You mean your best friend," the lady corrected and assessed Alicia with a cool gaze.

Best friend? Alicia didn't believe that a guy could be best friends with a girl; anyone who claimed that had undisclosed feelings toward the other person as far as she was concerned. She now noticed Laura had her arm linked with Blake's. Well, Blake had some explaining to do.

"Nice to meet you," Alicia said and extended her hand to shake Laura's, but the lady ignored it. Ouch.

"Laura is a first-year associate at one of the top corporate law firms in New York. A dream come true for her, right, Laura?" Blake said.

"You know me better than most," Laura responded with a smile.

Alicia sensed a long history between them. A history she wouldn't be able to penetrate. *Surely, today can't get any worse*, she reasoned.

As though sensing how awkward she felt, Josh announced a game of cards in which they would play in teams. Laura quickly grabbed Blake as her partner and dragged him over to the game table, but then changed the rules of the game and insisted on sitting next to Blake. Blake shot Alicia an apologetic look, which she pretended not to notice as she settled in next to Josh. It wasn't supposed to be a big deal, right?

But as the game progressed, Alicia could see this was not the first time Blake and Laura had played together—they were comfortable with each other and played in sync. Blake looked so excited and got more animated as the game went on. This was a part of him that Alicia had never seen before. A side that had only been brought to the surface by Laura.

Alicia felt like the third wheel but tried to

hide it. The group played a set of five games and the Blake-Laura team won them all. Blake and Laura high-fived each other, but it seemed Blake hadn't forgotten Alicia, because he came over to where she sat and gave her a big hug.

With the game over, all the guys moved back to the barbecue station to continue grilling the chicken, burgers, and corn cobs. Blake joined them as well. Alicia moved back to her reclining chair and sat down.

"He's good looking, right?" She turned to see Laura slide into the chair next to hers.

Alicia said nothing, opened her can of ginger ale, and took a sip. She wasn't really in the mood to engage in any conversation with Laura. *Could you go away already?* she thought.

"Blake and I have been best friends since we were little," Laura continued. "Everyone always assumed that we would get married to each other."

Alicia coughed and spilled her drink. Now she was getting ticked off. *You better stop, lady,* she thought.

But apparently, Laura didn't get the memo. She forged ahead. "Actually, the three of us were best friends," Laura continued, oblivious to Alicia's growing anger.

"Three?"

"You didn't know?" Laura cast her a surprised look. "Blake has a twin brother."

~

Time stood still for Alicia. "A twin brother?" she managed to say.

"Yes. Well, I should say he had one," Laura said. She had a faraway look on her face. "Henry was his best friend. We all grew up together. I remember our parents often called us the three musketeers. When Henry was eighteen years old, he died in a car accident. Blake was devastated. He lost both his brother and his best friend. He shut himself off, and it took him a long time to open up to people again. I was the only one who understood just how much Henry meant to him."

Alicia was still reeling from the news. Blake had never mentioned it. A twin brother, or any brother for that matter, was a big deal. Were Blake and her really as close as she had imagined? She had shared everything with him, but it seemed he had held a lot back. First Laura, and now Henry.

It was suddenly all too much. She needed to get away. The safest place seemed to be the bathroom. Alicia jumped up, grabbed her bag, and mumbled that she had to go to the restroom.

After spending a few minutes gathering her wits about her, she washed her hands and then went to look for Blake. It was time to speak with him. There was no sense in trying to make heads or tails of it on her own.

As Alicia walked toward the terrace, she heard voices coming from the direction of Blake's study. She glanced there and what she saw startled her beyond words.

Blake and Laura were facing each other and talking quietly. Then Alicia saw Laura reach out a hand and touch Blake's face for a moment, and then she hugged him. Blake did not step away, but hugged her right back.

Alicia felt like she had been slapped. She struggled to catch her breath, and tears filled her eyes.

Not wanting to stay another moment, she turned and fled the apartment.

CHAPTER 33

Laura leaned against Blake's desk. "I found someone." Laura beamed. "His name is Michael. We met at a company dinner for one of my clients, and we hit it off right away. We've been dating for a while. He gets me and makes me happy. Now, he wants to introduce me to his parents. I would love him to meet mine as well."

"That's great. What does he do?" Blake asked quietly.

"He works at a hedge fund. I never thought I would be able to let go of Henry." Laura traced her finger on the desk's surface. "Even now, I still miss him. But Michael is a great guy."

Blake stayed quiet. He could sense that

Laura yearned for some kind of approval from him. It was unfair to expect her to wait for someone who was already gone. "It would be great to meet him," he said finally.

She smiled. "Thank you." She folded her arms over her chest. "So, how are you doing? You seem happy," she said.

"I am." Just thinking about Alicia brought a smile to his face. He didn't remember when he had been this happy.

"Wow, you really like her, or should I say love her," Laura said. "I'm glad to see you opening your heart again. Does she know you like her this much?"

"No, I haven't told her."

"You should! She likes you too, you know. Make sure she doesn't get away." She straightened up and faced Blake. "It was great seeing you." She touched his face and gave him a hug.

Blake hugged her back. He would miss seeing Laura, but he was happy that Laura had found happiness. Now he needed to go look for his love.

Blake stepped away and left the study. He checked the terrace, but didn't see Alicia. He looked around the rest of the penthouse, but she was nowhere to be found. Josh came walking down the hallway. "Have you seen Alicia?" Blake asked him.

"I thought I saw her leaving," Josh responded.

"Leaving? Why?" Blake pulled his phone and called her number. It was switched off. He called again, and it went into voicemail. "I hope nothing is wrong. Josh, I need to go look for her," he said.

"Go. I'll take care of things here."

Blake grabbed his keys from where they rested in a corner of his kitchen countertop and headed out.

$\mathcal{A}$licia entered her apartment and headed straight for her room. She heard Jasmine calling her name, but she ignored her and slammed her door shut. She wanted—no, she needed—to be alone. She laid down on her bed and threw her phone beside her.

She heard a knock on her door. "Alicia, are you okay?" Jasmine asked.

Alicia couldn't speak. She was afraid she would start crying, and she didn't want to. She just wished Jasmine would go away.

The doorbell rang. Alicia heard Dana's voice as she answered the door. "What happened to Alicia?"

"I don't know. Is she in?" she heard Blake respond.

Alicia covered her head with the pillow. She wasn't ready to talk to him. Not yet.

"She's in her room," Dana said.

Alicia heard Blake's footfalls until he reached her door. He knocked. "Alicia, what's wrong? I looked for you and you were gone," Blake said.

Alicia sat up. "Leave me alone," she cried out.

"I don't understand. Is everything okay?" Alicia heard him lean against the door.

Of all the nerve. "Why did you come? Go back to your girlfriend," Alicia retorted.

"What girlfriend? I only know one, and she has even refused to be my girlfriend. For now."

"What about Laura? You were all cozy with her."

"Laura?" Blake laughed. "Laura has a boyfriend she's about to introduce to her parents."

Wait! What? Alicia sprung to her feet and cracked her door open to see Blake's face. "But I saw you ...."

Blake stepped in and shut her door behind him. He looked around. "Nice room." He turned his gaze back on Alicia. "As I was saying. Laura has a boyfriend; that's what she was telling me about." He folded his arms and looked at Alicia. "Laura used to be my brother's sweetheart."

"You didn't tell me you had a brother."

"Oh, I don't talk about him much. I'm sorry." Alicia flopped on the bed. "It's okay."

"So you were jealous." Blake sat on her bed.

"No, I wasn't." She tried to scoot away to the farthest part of the bed.

"Oh yes, you were." Blake grinned, grabbed her, and pulled her to him. "I'm glad you were jealous," he whispered.

It felt good to be in his arms. She had missed him. She had only known Blake for a few weeks, but he'd invaded her heart. She leaned her head on his shoulder.

Blake was quiet for a few moments. "Henry was my twin," he began. "We were best friends, and he was the funniest person I'd ever known. He was smart and outgoing. He truly loved people. He always wanted to be a lawyer. I, on the other hand, had no idea what I wanted to be."

Blake's hand rubbed her cheek. It was a light

feathery touch that sent sparks all over Alicia's nerve endings. Alicia leaned closer to him.

"When we were eighteen, I had a girlfriend, Miranda, who at the time seemed to like Henry. And I was the only one who didn't know. She only considered me because there were rumors around town that I was inheriting all the family fortune, not Henry. Laura was Henry's sweetheart at the time. My brother got a call from Miranda that she was in a bad situation, and she couldn't reach me. Unknown to me, Miranda had switched off my phone before heading out and calling my brother. Henry tried to reach me but couldn't. So he called Laura and told her what was happening and that he was going to pick Miranda up on my behalf. On his way, he had a car accident and died. I found out later from Laura what had happened. And it was on the day before our birthday."

"When is your birthday?"

"November twentieth." Henry's death anniversary was coming up in a few days. Alicia didn't know what to say. She hugged him tighter.

Blake's voice broke as he continued. "When he died, my world fell apart. It was like a piece of me had died. I couldn't function for months, and Laura was the only one who could reach me. She loved Henry, and she understood how devastated I was. She would sit with me day in and day out and say nothing. We cried together and mourned him. Eventually, we started to live again. And I knew Henry would want me to make sure Laura was okay." He tightened his hold on Alicia.

"You still miss him," Alicia said.

"Yes." Alicia held him tightly and rubbed her hand down his back. "That's why I can't afford to lose you or any other person I care for," Blake said quietly.

Alicia lifted her head and looked into his eyes. "You won't."

They stared at each other. Alicia's heart raced. It was like all the air in the room had been sucked out. Blake brushed his fingers over her cheek, and Alicia's breath hitched. Her heart now pounded with the possibility that he might kiss her. His face moved closer, his lips a mere whisper away. And when he touched her other cheek, Alicia forgot her name. Soft hints of his woody mint scent enveloped her until it became all she could breathe in. And then he kissed her.

It was soft at first and tender like the brush of a butterfly's wings, and then he deepened the kiss, flooding her whole body with light, warmth, and happiness. Driving all her emotional pain away and leaving sweetness behind.

All too soon, Blake ended the kiss and rested his forehead on hers. "I think I need to go, my sweet jewel," he said with a ragged breath.

Alicia understood immediately. He wanted to leave to protect her.

Her heart did a somersault.

CHAPTER 35

"I think that's it. Miss Rosa, you are going to be just fine." Even though it was Sunday evening and she wasn't on-call, Alicia had come to the hospital to see the newly admitted patients. Miss Rosa was one of them.

"What did you say?" Miss Rosa was an octogenarian who had arrived at the ER with cough and fever. She'd been diagnosed with pneumonia and, given her age, had also been kept on for close monitoring. And she had difficulty with her hearing.

"You are going to be just fine," Alicia said loudly.

"I can hear you. You don't have to shout," Miss Rosa replied.

Alicia exchanged a smile with the intern. This was something her own grandmother would have said. "Okay, Miss Rosa. I'll come and see you tomorrow."

"My dear, could you make sure that cute nurse is the one that comes to check up on me? You know, the male nurse with the nice smile?"

Alicia's lips twitched upward in a smile. "I'll see what I can do."

"Thank you, dear. Now, where is the remote?" Miss Rosa picked up the remote and started flipping channels until she found the soap opera she wanted.

Alicia left her laughing to the drama that was playing out on the screen. She met the nurse-on-duty in the hallway outside Miss Rosa's room. "Any requests from Miss Rosa?" the nurse asked.

"She wants Miguel to check up on her."

"No can do. Every time Miguel checks her, her heart rate goes really high. I wonder what she's always fantasizing about when she sees him. Even though he doesn't vocalize it, the poor boy is traumatized since Miss Rosa is always trying to feel out his muscles."

Alicia couldn't help laughing. "I know this

isn't funny, but Miguel was always bragging how he was a chick magnet. Well, Miss Rosa is a chick alright."

"Oh, he has eaten some humble pie. And she is so sweet and means no harm, so there's really not much we can do. I'll get one of the other nurses to check on her."

"Thanks."

"You're welcome."

Alicia chuckled as she walked away. One thing was certain—the hospital was never boring.

Her phone buzzed. Alicia checked the screen and saw that it was a text message from Josh. He was waiting for her in the hospital lobby.

Her pace quickened. When she'd woken up this morning, she could still feel the imprint of Blake's kiss on her lips. The kiss had been everything and more than she expected. But what had touched her the most had been his self-restraint to make sure they never went beyond a kiss.

And she had remembered he'd mentioned that his birthday was on November twentieth. She wanted to plan a memorable one for him this year, one that celebrated Henry's life too. Because Henry was a part of who Blake was—he was his past and part of his motivation for the future. She had reached out to Josh to help her plan it. Josh would know what Blake liked.

She made it to the hospital lobby in record time. She saw Josh leaning against the information desk, talking to the cute front desk receptionist-on-duty. She could see the receptionist was blushing. Now here was another chick magnet.

"Hello, Josh," Alicia said.

"Hey, Alicia." He turned to the receptionist and flashed a brilliant smile. "It was great talking to you, Maggie. See you some other time." Maggie smiled back. He gestured to Alicia to lead the way. "Let's go."

"Thanks for meeting me," Alicia said as they walked out of the hospital. The air was cool, and the streets were somewhat empty. Alicia was glad she didn't need a jacket yet.

"It was no problem. I was already at the hospital for a consult. I'll come back later tonight once we are done. You are headed home, right?"

"Yes."

"Since it's getting late, why don't I walk you home and we can talk on the way?"

"Sounds perfect."

"So how can I help you? You said something about Blake's birthday."

"Yes. Blake told me yesterday that his birthday is on November twentieth."

"It is, and he never celebrates it."

"Because of Henry."

"He told you about Henry? Yes, it reminds him too much about the loss, and he feels guilty about being happy on his birthday when Henry isn't there."

"What if we celebrated Henry as well instead? I'm thinking having the birthday at some restaurant that Blake likes, but also showing a compilation of some pictures or videos of Henry and Blake together, reminding Blake of the good times they had. You know, make the birthday about the two of them."

"I think that's a great idea. Blake likes this restaurant called Miggiano. Have you heard about it?"

"The new place that opened about six months ago? I've heard that it has a reservation list that is about a mile long."

"Don't worry about that. I can get us in. The

owner of the restaurant owes me a favor. We'll probably need the whole day, right?"

"You mean reserve the whole restaurant for the whole day? That would be so expensive!"

"That's not a problem. Like I said, the owner owes me a favor. It's not a big deal. Consider it done."

Alicia didn't know what to say. Blake and Josh seemed to move on another level, a world that was very different from the one she knew. She was still getting used to it. "Okay. Let's talk invite list."

The conversation flowed easily between them as they walked to her house. Alicia discovered that Josh was a soccer fan and was even part-owner of one of the European football clubs. She'd just thought he was a doctor at the hospital, but it seemed he was so much more. He told her a bit about all the antics Blake and he had gotten into growing up, and by the time they reached the front of her house, Alicia couldn't remember when she had laughed so hard. She held her side from the stitch she now felt.

Josh touched her arm. "Are you okay?" he said, his brow furrowed.

Alicia smiled at him. "I'm fine. I just have a stitch in my side from all the laughter. Thanks for walking me home."

"My pleasure. Now I see why Blake likes you so much. You are good for him."

"Why, thank you."

"Okay, I'll take care of the restaurant and the invites. And I'll talk to his mom about the pictures and videos. I'll get those to you tomorrow."

"Sounds good. Thanks again for all your help."

"I can't wait to see Blake's face. And I'll probably add a prank or two to the party."

"Don't you dare!"

Josh laughed. "I was just joking. Not."

Alicia put her hands on her hips. "Josh, I'm serious. Don't you dare mess this up."

Josh held up his hands in mock surrender. "Okay, okay, mademoiselle."

Alicia smiled. "Alright. I'll hold you to it."

Her phone buzzed, and then she heard a familiar tune coming from it. One she hadn't heard in a while.

Alicia froze, and her heart skipped a beat.

CHAPTER 36

*B*lake whistled as he drove over to Alicia's house. He'd just come from the jewelry store. Yesterday with Alicia had been wonderful. And the kiss had been the icing on the cake. After he'd left her place, he had called her when he got home, and they'd spent the rest of the evening chatting and laughing on the phone.

He'd felt so alive, like he'd found what was missing in his life. He wondered how he had managed before meeting her. And when he couldn't sleep—his mind was preoccupied with thoughts of her—he'd gone online and signed up for a subscription service to watch some Korean dramas. And Alicia had been right—

they were funny and engaging. He'd also noticed that the men liked to give the ladies a couple's ring, which had given him an idea.

He'd called their family jeweler, who informed him that he had a set that might just meet his needs and he would have it ready for him the next day. Blake had gone this evening to the store and picked up the simple white gold bands that had "I love you" inscribed in Korean all around them. One for Alicia and one for him. He'd guesstimated Alicia's ring size, and they could always have it adjusted if it didn't fit.

He patted the ring box in his pocket and looked at the lilac bouquet on the passenger seat. Alicia would be pleased. He had the scenario all planned out for how he would give her the ring. He didn't mind wearing his own as well. It would be a signal that he was off the market. Which was true because he had finally accepted what had been staring him in the face —Alicia could be the one. The woman he hadn't known he'd been searching for his whole life.

He spotted Alicia's house up ahead. As he drew closer, he noticed her standing on the front steps. Awesome. He had wanted to surprise her, and this would make it easy. But wait, who was it standing next to her and making her laugh so hard?

Blake pressed the brake suddenly. He couldn't believe what he was seeing. What was Josh doing here? And why was he standing in front of Alicia's house? He saw Josh say something to Alicia, and she laughed. And then Josh touched Alicia, and Alicia smiled back at him.

Blake felt a stab in his heart and he almost doubled over. It was like Miranda all over again. How could they—his best friend and the girl he liked—do this to him? He'd thought Alicia was different, but it seemed he had been wrong, dead wrong.

His heart squeezed in pain, and Blake gasped. He needed to leave, go somewhere he could breathe again. He couldn't stay here and watch the betrayal continue before his eyes. And he knew just the right place.

Blake put his car into drive and drove off, his tires screeching into the night.

CHAPTER 37

Alicia's heart started beating loudly. No, no, it couldn't be happening again! She felt a hand touch her and saw Josh looking at her with concern. "Are you okay?" he asked.

"Yes … yes, I'm fine." She remembered where she was. "I need to take this call." She reached into her bag and pulled out her phone. She pressed the answer button.

"This is Alicia," she said.

"Hi, it's Nurse Hamilton from Dexington Medical Center's Pediatric Unit," the person on the other end of the line said. "It's Willow. I'm afraid you need to come to the hospital."

CHAPTER 38

Alicia rushed into the hospital with Josh in tow. She'd told him about the call and who Willow was to her. Alicia headed straight to Willow's room. A nurse met her outside the entrance. "How is Willow?" she asked as she wrung her hands.

"She's been moved to the PICU," the nurse said. "I'm sorry."

Alicia raced down the hallway and took the elevator to the Pediatric Intensive Care Unit. Josh followed her. "She'll be alright," he said.

Alicia was glad Josh was with her, but she wished Blake was the one with her instead. "Have you been able to reach Blake?" she asked.

She had tried his number on their way to the hospital, but it had gone straight to voicemail.

"No, it's still switched off. I wonder where he is."

Alicia knew she couldn't think about Blake now. Willow was in trouble and that was all she needed to focus on. *Please, darling, be okay. Help her, God*, she prayed. Willow had seemed okay yesterday. She wondered what could have happened.

The elevator pinged, and they stepped out. Alicia rushed into the PICU and met the nurse at the central station. "I'm here about Willow Rushford."

"And you are?"

"I'm Alicia Montgomery, her aunt and her guardian." Alicia showed the nurse her hospital ID.

The nurse typed into the computer in front of her. "Let me page the doctor-on-call," she said. The nurse picked up the phone in front of her and made a call.

Alicia's heart sank like it was a boulder. It must be bad if the nurse had to call the doctor to speak to her. She gripped the edge of the station counter. *Keep it together, Alicia,* she told herself. Willow needed her.

"Dr. Montgomery." Alicia turned at the sound of her name to see Dr. Alex Baird. He was a well-known pediatric intensivist and a member of the cystic fibrosis team at the hospital. He had been in charge of Willow's case on previous occasions—Willow was in good hands.

"Dr. Baird, how is she doing?" Alicia wrung her hands.

"She was having trouble breathing, but seems to be stabilizing a bit now," Dr. Baird said. "We found a lot of mucus in her lungs, and we have no idea what triggered it. We've suctioned out as much as we can and placed her on a cocktail of drugs to help counteract it. And it seems to be working. She is on a respirator now, and has a tube draining from her side. We'd like to keep her here for observation for the next twenty-four hours before moving her back to the ward. Would you like to see her?"

The nurse gave Alicia a gown, cap, mask, and booties, which she donned. She followed after Dr. Baird until she remembered that Josh was still with her. She turned to look at him, and he waved her forward. She gave him a wry smile, but then realized that he couldn't see it with her mask on. She turned back and walked through the open glass door of Willow's PICU cubicle, which then swooshed closed behind her.

Willow looked tiny and vulnerable on the bed. A tube snaked into her mouth, held in place by narrow strips of tape. A respirator mask was placed over her nose and mouth, and an IV line ran from a vein on her left arm. Her chest rose and fell in rhythm with the sounds from the bedside monitors. Another tube extended from the side of her chest into a glass reservoir on the floor that was a quarter-filled with a pink-tinged mucous fluid.

"I'm glad we were able to catch it in time," Dr. Baird said. "If we had waited five minutes, it might have been too late."

Alicia held back a whimper. She moved to Willow's right side and held her limp hand in hers. "I'm here, Willow. You'll be alright."

"Why don't I give you a few minutes with her?" Dr. Baird said.

Alicia threw him an appreciative glance and then focused back on Willow. She heard the glass door open and close as Dr. Baird went out.

"I'm here, darling. Mummy is here," Alicia whispered with a choking voice. She didn't know when tears started streaming down her face. She was the cause of everything. If not for her choice, Willow wouldn't have the cystic fibrosis gene that made her life so difficult. She swallowed another cry. Why did Willow have to suffer for her mistakes? She laid her head on Willow's bed as she continued to hold Willow's hand in hers. She lost track of how long she stayed that way.

She felt a hand on her head. She looked up to see Willow's eyes wide open. Willow tried to speak, but all Alicia could hear was a gargled sound. "It's okay," she patted Willow's hand reassuringly. "Don't try to speak. You have a tube in your mouth." Alicia reached up and pressed the call button.

After a few moments, the nurse walked in. "Oh, she is awake. Let me get the doctor." She walked out and then walked back in with Dr. Baird.

Dr. Baird picked up the chart from the foot of the bed. "I can see the tube is no longer draining. There is no change in the fluid quantity from the last check." He stepped to Willow and listened to her chest. "Her lungs seem clear."

Alicia let out a deep exhale. She hadn't realized she was holding her breath.

Dr. Baird turned to the nurse. "Let's remove the nasopharyngeal tube and see if she can breathe on her own."

The nurse donned a pair of gloves and walked to the head of Willow's bed. With quick movements, she removed the tube and dumped it into a metal tray.

Willow tried to speak again, but only a croak emerged. Dr. Baird gave her a smile. "Willow, take your time. You've been through a lot, but you've been a champ through it all." He listened to Willow's chest again. "She's breathing on her own, and her lungs are still clear. We'll observe her for a few hours, but it's safe to say that we may move her earlier than we expected." Then Dr. Baird gestured in the direction of the door.

"I'll be back, sweetie." Alicia gave Willow's hand a reassuring squeeze. She followed Dr. Baird outside the room.

"We are glad Willow is now doing okay, but this was a really bad episode," Dr. Baird said. "I've talked to some of my peers about it, and we think it may have been triggered by the cool weather. She has been doing really well on the treatment protocol, and the last thing we need is for her to relapse. Do you think it would be possible to move her to a warmer climate till she finishes her treatment?"

Alicia thought for a moment. Then she remembered Carol, her sister's friend, who had been inviting her since forever to come to Florida. "I think I have someone we can stay with in Florida, but I would need to talk to her before confirming any plans."

"Florida. That would be perfect. We are also running the treatment trial at Florida State Hospital, so it would be easy to have Willow join the program there and still complete the treatment."

"Okay. Let me get back to you about it tomorrow. Thanks for taking care of Willow."

"Glad to help, but Willow did most of the work. She is a fighter. See you later." Dr. Baird walked away toward the nurses' station.

"How is she doing?"

Alicia jumped at the voice and turned to see Josh. "You scared me!"

"Sorry," Josh said with a sheepish grin on his face.

"I thought you had left."

"I wanted to make sure she was okay before leaving."

Alicia was touched. She could see why Josh was Blake's best friend—he was just as compassionate as Blake was. "She's doing much better. They might move her back to the wards in a few hours."

"That's great."

Alicia noticed Josh couldn't look her in the eye. "What's wrong? Spill it out already," Alicia said.

He ran a hand through his hair. "It seems Blake has left town for the weekend."

"How did you …?"

"He left a message for Laura and his mom."

And he didn't leave one for me, she completed silently. Alicia didn't understand why, but it seemed Blake had bailed on her. Tears welled up behind her eyelids and threatened to run down her face. She couldn't allow Josh to see her like this. She turned her face away.

"Alicia …"

"It doesn't matter. I have to go back in. Thanks for letting me know, Josh."

Her shoulders slumped, Alicia walked back into Willow's cubicle and left Josh standing in the hallway.

CHAPTER 39

Blake picked up his bag from the car's passenger seat and slammed the door shut. He'd spent the last three days at the family's summer cottage. It had always been a good place to clear his thoughts, but he wasn't sure how effective it had been this time around. He needed to pick up his mail so he walked across the garage and took the elevator to the lobby. His phone rang.

"Where are you?" Josh said on the other end of the line.

"I just got home."

"I'm coming over." Josh ended the call.

What was that all about? Anyway, it was a good thing Josh was coming. They needed to talk. He still couldn't believe that Josh could betray him like that.

Blake collected his mail and rode the elevator to his floor. He stepped into his apartment, and the sweet smell of lilac hit his nose. It was like a punch to his stomach and negated the three days he had spent trying to erase thoughts of her. He'd forgotten about the bouquet.

He dropped his car keys and bag on the kitchen counter and looked at the wilted flowers lying there. Just like his love had wilted. He picked them up and shoved them into the trashcan.

Then he headed to the bathroom to take a quick shower before Josh arrived.

Maybe the shower would help quiet the urge to run to Alicia.

Blake heard the chime of the elevator doors as they opened to reveal Josh wearing a frown on his face. He turned and walked back into the apartment, expecting Josh to follow. He sat down on the couch and crossed his legs.

"How could you?" Josh said, his face furious.

"How could I what? You have some nerve showing your face here."

"What?" His face mirrored his confusion. "What are you talking about?"

Blake stood up. "How could you do this to me, Josh? You've been my friend since childhood, and I trusted you."

"What the hell are you talking about?"

"Don't pretend. I saw you and Alicia in front of her house, laughing and having fun together."

"Are you for real? Is that why you bailed on Alicia when she needed you the most?"

Blake's heart raced. "What are you talking about?"

"Blake, I didn't know you were such a jerk. Alicia wanted to surprise you for your birthday and asked me to plan your birthday with her. I met her at the hospital and since it was late, I walked her home. We were laughing about how great it would be to see your surprised face. You can call Miggiano to confirm the reservation I already made for your birthday as part of the plans. It's your favorite restaurant after all."

Blake flopped on the couch. "I didn't know."

"So you took off instead of asking her? For goodness sake, she is not Miranda!"

Blake held his head in his hands. "What have I done?"

"And while you were running off by yourself, her niece Willow had a crisis and almost died."

Blake's head whipped up. "What?"

"You heard me. Alicia was looking for you, but you were nowhere to be found. And then she found out you told Laura and your mom where you went but didn't tell her. How do you think she felt?"

Blake's head fell back down on his hands. "I've messed up."

"Big time," Josh agreed.

Blake jumped up. "I need to go see her."

"I'm just going to stay right here and watch TV. Good luck."

"Thanks. I need it." Blake picked up his car keys from the kitchen countertop and rushed out of the apartment.

CHAPTER 40

"I'll miss you," Dana said.

"I'll miss you too." Alicia closed her small carry-on bag and gave Dana a hug. They were standing in Alicia's bedroom.

Alicia looked around. She would miss this place. But she would be back soon once Willow got better. She had gotten a month's leave with permission from Dr. Hartwood. But she wouldn't be idle in Florida.

Dr. Kim had arranged with Dr. Hartwood for Alicia's research rotation to take place immediately, so her residency program wouldn't be affected by the move. She would be working with one of Dr. Kim's collaborators on genetic research, a professor at Florida State Hospital, the same hospital where Willow would be receiving her treatment. Willow would be airlifted to the Florida hospital, and Alicia would be going with them.

Carol had been excited about having Willow and Alicia over at her house. She would be waiting for them at the hospital in Florida. Everything was all set except for the one issue she needed to take care of—Blake.

Alicia had stayed an extra day hoping that Blake would come and see her. She had even caved in and called his number, but his phone had been switched off. Blake hadn't called her back and hadn't come to visit. It seemed he no longer wanted anything to do with her. She had to let him go.

She sighed, picked up her bag, and stepped into the living room. Jasmine was standing by the dining table. "Call us when you get in," Jasmine said.

"I will." Alicia gave Jasmine a hug. "Please don't tell Blake where I went."

"Alicia, don't you think you guys need to talk?" Dana chimed in.

"It's over. There is nothing else to talk

about." Alicia gave them both a rueful smile. "I need to focus on Willow for now."

She walked over to the door and opened it. "I'll see you guys in a month's time." She shut the door behind her and stepped into the cab waiting outside.

Then the cab drove away.

CHAPTER 41

"Who is it?" Jasmine opened the door to see Blake standing outside. "You have some nerve coming here," she accused Blake.

"Can I come in?" Blake asked.

"No, you can't." Jasmine stepped out onto the front steps and closed the door behind her.

"Can you tell Alicia I'm here?"

"No can do. Alicia is gone."

"Gone?"

"Yes, gone. Did you think she would be waiting for you? How could you do this to her?" Jasmine's eyes flashed with anger.

"I didn't know the truth."

"And you didn't think you needed to talk to

her to find out? You really hurt her, Blake. I've never seen her like this before."

Blake was gutted. He didn't know what to do. "I'm sorry," he said.

"I'm not the one you should tell."

"She's not picking up my calls."

"It's too late, Blake. You should go." Jasmine opened the door and stepped back in.

"Wait! Where is she?"

"Somewhere she doesn't want you."

Jasmine slammed the door in his face.

CHAPTER 42

The light from the suddenly opened curtains hurt his eyes. "Aargh." He shielded his eyes with his hand as he turned away from the windows. He had taken a leave from the hospital since Alicia left and had been staying at his parents' house ever since.

Everything at his own home reminded him of Alicia, and his heart couldn't take it any longer. His family had pretty much left him alone, but he'd known they would intervene very soon. He just hadn't expected it to be today. He removed his hand from his eyes to see his mom standing before him with her hands on her hips.

She pointed at him. "You need to go."

"Go?" Blake couldn't understand what his mom was talking about. He sat up on the bed. His head hurt, and his tongue felt like lead.

"You need to go look for Alicia. You look terrible. I'm tired of you moping around the house." Sarah glanced around and wrinkled her nose. "And this place looks and smells like a pigsty."

"Mom, leave me alone." Blake fell back on the bed and covered himself with the duvet.

"Oh no, you don't!" Sarah snatched the duvet away.

"M-o-m!"

"You're right. I'm your mom, and I want my son back." Sarah sat at the edge of the bed and faced Blake. "You love her, right?" Blake nodded.

"And you miss her?"

"More than I ever thought possible." Blake realized that the loss he felt was like when Henry died. There was like a gaping hole where his heart used to be. He wasn't sure how long he would survive without her. He missed her terribly.

"Then go fight for her."

"I'm not sure she feels the same way," he said.

"Well, you won't know by moping around here. Even your father is worried about you." Blake looked at his mom in disbelief. "Your father may not say it, but I know him more than he knows himself. He hasn't been sleeping well at night because of you," Sarah responded with a smile. "You are used to going after everything you want. Why are you holding back?"

Why indeed? And then the truth hit him. He was afraid of being rejected. But losing Alicia permanently would probably kill him. At least this way, he still had a chance.

"Thanks, Mom!" Blake leaned forward and gave her a kiss and a hug and then jumped out of bed, leaving a stunned Sarah staring at him. Blake grinned at her and rushed into the bathroom.

"Make sure you shave that five o'clock beard!" Sarah called after him. "There's no need to look like a caveman."

Blake grimaced at his view in the mirror. He would clean up first and then go look for Alicia.

He now knew what to do.

Blake walked up the stairs leading to Alicia's house. He patted the box in his inner jacket pocket. He had picked a ring that he thought Alicia would like—simple, understated, but still elegant. The family jeweler had told him this was a new line that just came into the store and was the only one of its kind. Just like Alicia.

Blake rang the doorbell. Dana opened the door. She had a headband on her head and was wearing a yellow tank top with grey shorts. It looked like she had been working out.

"Blake," Dana said.

"Dana," Blake responded.

Dana sighed and opened the door for him to come in.

Blake stepped in and looked around. The living room looked the same, but it wasn't. Alicia wasn't there.

Dana walked to the kitchen and opened the refrigerator to grab a bottle of water. She closed its door and turned to him. "You know she is not here," she said.

"Dana, I'm sure Alicia must have left some

information with you. Please tell me where she is," Blake implored.

"I don't know, Blake."

"Please, Dana." Blake opened his jacket and brought out the box. "I'm serious about her. Please help me not to lose her."

Dana stared at the box, and then at Blake, then back at the box. She sighed. "Okay. But you can't mess this up."

"I won't." Blake's heart rate picked up. He still had a chance.

Dana walked back to the fridge and grabbed a piece of paper held down by a magnet. "This is the address. She gave it to me to forward any critical mail to her." She extended the paper to Blake.

Blake accepted the paper, pulled out his phone, and took a picture of it. "Thanks, Dana." He handed the paper back to her and sprinted out of the house. He called his pilot to ready the jet.

It was time to head to Florida.

CHAPTER 43

Alicia looked out at the waves from her chair on the porch as they rolled in and then out. The sound of billowing waves mixed with the call of seagulls filled the air. Carol's beachfront house had an amazing view, and she could see why Carol loved it here. Even Willow had adjusted well. She had improved so much that she was allowed to take brief walks along the beachfront, something she had never been able to do before. The experimental treatment was working wonders, and some days it seemed so unreal. Alicia was grateful.

Carol had also been wonderful. She had stepped into the role of big sister easily and had eased Alicia's ache from missing her sister. It wasn't surprising given that Carol had been Mary's best friend. And she loved Willow like she was her own child. Everything seemed perfect, but Alicia knew something was absent.

Blake. She missed him. She knew she should feel better about her decision to leave him behind, but that didn't stop her from thinking about him all the time. She could hear his laughter, remember his little teasing jabs at her, and recall the warmth in his eyes that served as windows into his soul.

She missed his touch that both excited and calmed her. And their talks that made her lose track of time. He'd understood her, hadn't judged her, and had accepted her for who she was. Fine, she'd been angry about his disappearance when she needed him most, but she'd never found out why, neither had she given him the chance to explain. It had been wrong to cut him off just like that.

Alicia felt a hand touch her. She turned to see Carol settle into the chair next to her, her short blonde curls blown everywhere by the wind.

"Willow is asleep. The trip to Disney World sure wore her out." Carol had offered to help

Willow take a bath and subsequently get her to take a nap.

"She had a great time. Thanks for taking us there."

"I think I had more fun than you two."

Alicia knew that Carol wished that she had a child of her own. Her fiancé had been killed in Afghanistan on his second tour of duty, and Carol could not imagine marrying anyone else yet.

"So what's on your mind? Are you thinking about Blake?" Carol asked.

Alicia looked sharply at her. "How did you …?"

"Willow told me. She says you call his name in your sleep." Alicia had chosen to sleep with Willow every night, even though Willow had her own room. She loved to tell her bedtime stories and snuggle with her. She'd never had the chance to do that before.

Alicia said nothing. She stared out at the beach without looking at anything in particular.

"Do you want to talk about it?" Carol said softly.

Alicia didn't know when she started crying. It was like a dam broke within her. Carol hugged her and rubbed her back. Before she knew it, she had told Carol about how she'd met him and how she'd left him.

"I didn't realize how much I loved him. How can I love someone I only met a few weeks ago?" Alicia said, sniffling.

"I loved Patrick, my fiancé, the first day I met him," Carol said. "And that only grew the more I found out who he truly was. Does Blake know how much you love him?"

"No, he doesn't. I don't even know if he feels the same way. I mean, I know he likes me, but that's not the same thing as love. What if he disappears when he finds out how I feel? I don't want a repeat of what happened before."

"Why would he leave you? Not everybody is like Charles."

Alicia's eyes widened. "You know about him?"

"Yes, Mary told me. I know Willow is your daughter. We agreed that I would take care of you both if anything ever happened to her."

Alicia now understood why Carol had kept in touch with her regularly and always wanted to know how she was doing. She didn't know what she had done to deserve her love.

"Has Blake ever given you any indication that he would abandon you?" Carol asked.

"No. But I'm afraid that he may not be able to accept both Willow and me."

"Does he know about Willow?"

"Yes, he knows she's my daughter."

"Did his behavior change after he found out?"

"No."

"So give him a chance. How can you know if he would accept Willow if you don't let him try?"

Alicia leaned back on the chair. What Carol said made a lot of sense. Maybe she should give him a chance.

The sound of the doorbell echoed out to the porch.

"I'll get it," Carol said. She got up and walked into the house.

Alicia could hear the front door opening and Carol talking to someone at the door. She closed her eyes. She needed some time alone to think about what Carol had said.

"Alicia." She would recognize that voice anywhere. Her eyes shot open. *It's not possible,* she thought. But it was. Blake was standing in front of her, wearing a button-down blue shirt with rolled up sleeves and blue jeans. The picture of perfection.

"What are you doing here?"

"Alicia, I ..."

"Alicia, who is this handsome young man?" Carol cut in.

"Blake, meet Carol, my sister's best friend. Carol meet Blake," Alicia answered.

Carol stretched out her hand for a handshake. Blake took her hand in his. "So, you are the Blake," she said as she shook his hand. "I've heard so much about you. Willow didn't exaggerate," Carol said, giving him an appreciative once-over.

Alicia could see Blake's ears turning red. That brought the hint of a smile to her lips.

"I'll leave you guys to chat. Remember, Alicia, a chance." Carol winked and left them.

"What chance?" Blake said, turning back to Alicia.

"Nothing. What are you doing here?"

"Can we take a walk?" Blake held out his hand to her.

Alicia ignored it and got up on her own. She started walking toward the beach, and Blake followed her. They strolled for a few minutes in silence. Blake stopped and touched her arm. Alicia turned to him.

"How is Willow?" Blake asked.

"She is doing great. She is taking a nap now."

"I'm glad she is doing well." Blake fidgeted with his hands. Taking a deep breath, he looked straight at Alicia. "Alicia, I'm sorry for not being there for you when you needed me."

Alicia said nothing. She looked away at the horizon.

Blake touched her arm again, and Alicia felt her walls tumbling down. "I thought you had something with Josh. I was on my way over to see you when I saw you laughing and giggling with him. It was like Miranda all over again. I couldn't stay, so I left town for a few days to clear my head. By the time I came back to talk to you about it, you had left."

Alicia now understood why he hadn't been

available. "You hurt me, Blake. You should have come to me first instead of assuming."

"I'm really sorry, Alicia. I shouldn't have allowed my experience with Miranda cloud my judgement about who I knew you were. You are nothing like her."

"I'm sorry too."

"For what?"

"For leaving town without giving you a way to reach me."

"From now on, I promise to be open with you about everything and work out any differences we have together."

"I promise too."

Blake hugged her. It felt incredible to be back in his arms. This was where she belonged.

"I missed you," Blake said.

Alicia smiled and looked into his eyes. "I missed you too."

"Can you give me a chance to make it up to you?"

Alicia nodded. She wasn't going anywhere. Blake was the man for her.

"Blakey!" a small voice cried out.

Alicia and Blake turned to see Willow by the

back door, dressed in a Mickey Mouse shirt and shorts and rubbing her eyes.

Blake opened his arms, and Willow ran into them. Then he twirled her around. Willow's laughter filled the air, a musical note that Alicia never got tired of listening to. Blake put her down and stooped down to look at her.

"Willow, I have a serious question for you." Willow looked at him with expectant eyes. Blake got down on one knee and pulled out a box from his pants pocket. He opened it to reveal a beautiful diamond ring.

Alicia gasped. The ring was stunning—it featured a central diamond piece surrounded by seven smaller ones. "Willow, would you grant me permission to marry Alicia?" Blake asked.

Alicia stood still in shock. This was the last thing she'd expected.

"Yes!" Willow shouted. Blake gave her a peck on the cheek. He turned to Alicia and held the ring out to her. Tears welled up in Alicia's eyes. She couldn't breathe.

"Alicia, I love you, and I can't imagine life without you and Willow. These past few days have made me realize how much you both are a part of my life. You are the most brilliant, sweet, and special woman I've ever met, and I would consider it an honor to spend the rest of my life with you. Would you marry me?"

Alicia couldn't think of what else to say. Hope and joy blossomed in her heart as she stared at the man she had come to love. "Yes."

Blake took her hand and put the ring on her finger. He grabbed her and kissed her soundly. Alicia felt the tingles of the kiss all the way to her toes.

Willow chuckled. Blake swept them both into his arms and twirled them around. The sounds of laughter echoed everywhere.

She had come home.

CHAPTER 44

Blake opened the door of the family mansion and ushered Alicia and Willow in. Alicia was dressed in a cream sweater over a blue flowery dress that somewhat matched Willow's frock. Alicia rubbed her hands down her dress, and the corners of her lips lifted when she saw both rings on her finger. Blake had given her the couple's ring once she had returned to Dexington.

"Blake, are you sure I look okay?" Alicia cast a worried glance at him.

"You look perfect."

Alicia could see the love in Blake's eyes. She smiled and raised her chin. "Okay, here we go." Willow giggled.

Blake held Willow's hand as they stepped into the house. Phillip and Sarah were sitting on the main couch and looked up to see them.

"Mom, Dad …" Blake began.

"Why don't we all take a seat?" Sarah said. She smiled approvingly at Blake.

Blake, Alicia, and Willow sat on the other couch. "Mom, Dad, I love Alicia, and I would like to spend the rest of my life with her."

Blake's father remained silent for a minute and then got up. Alicia's heart raced fast, and she waited with bated breath. He looked down at Blake and then smiled. "It's about time," he said. He picked up a document that had been lying beside him and headed to his study.

Alicia let out an exhale, and her shoulders relaxed.

Blake looked at his mother in amazement. "Your father and I had already discussed it," his mom said. "He knew you loved her, and was just waiting for your brain to catch up with your heart." Sarah turned to Alicia. "Welcome to the family." She got up from the couch, walked over to where Willow sat, and crouched at her level. "I'm happy to meet my cute grand-daughter." She smiled at Willow and opened her arms. Willow giggled and stepped into her embrace.

Alicia could barely hold back the tears.

Now she knew for certain everything was going to be okay.

EPILOGUE

"*How* is she?" Alicia asked and rubbed her hands together. She looked at the books behind the doctor's head and wished they could tell her the results already.

Dr. King peered down his glasses at her and leaned back in his chair. "The treatment has been very effective. We believe that Willow should not have any problems living a full active life from now on. I only need to see her once a year for a complete checkup barring any problems."

Alicia heaved a sigh of relief and looked at Blake. Blake beamed. He had been gripping her hand in anticipation of the news.

"I hear congratulations are in order," Dr. King said.

Alicia felt her face heat up. She still couldn't get used to hearing the warm wishes from doctors and nurses across the hospital.

"Thank you," Blake and Alicia responded in unison.

As they stepped out of the doctor's office into the hallway, Blake turned to Alicia. "I have a present for you." He handed her a large brown envelope.

What could this be? She opened it, pulled out a document, and looked in shock at Blake.

"This is the filing to commence Willow's adoption that the family lawyer submitted. I'll like Willow to officially be our daughter on the day we marry." Blake smiled at her.

Alicia's eyes filled with tears. This man standing in front of her was truly a godsent gift that she didn't deserve.

"Don't cry yet," Blake said. Alicia laughed through her tears. "I have something else for you." He handed Alicia a white envelope.

Alicia opened it to see a folded sheet of paper. She unfurled it and gasped. It was a genetic test report.

"I thought you might just want the peace of mind," Blake said. "I'm not a carrier for the cystic fibrosis gene. And even if I was, I'm fine with adoption if that's what you would prefer." Alicia could see the love shining from his eyes. "Because it is only you that I want as my wife."

"I love you," she mouthed and hugged him.

"I love you too, soon-to-be Alicia Dexington." Blake pulled her into a hug and gave her a kiss that melted Alicia's insides and curled her toes. A wonderful kiss from the man who loved her wholeheartedly and unreservedly.

Her own Billionaire Heir Doc.

Alicia ignored the clapping and catcalls from the patients waiting to see the doctor and kissed him right back.

Thank you so much for reading! Want to know what happens next in Dexington, and how Josh, Blake's friend, finds love (a fake fiancée romance)?

Check out LOVING THE BILLIONAIRE OWNER DOC at https://dobidaniels.com.

Here's an excerpt:

Warm light brown eyes with amber flecks stared back at her from a lightly stubbled face. Money was written all over him, from his tousled dark brown hair to his Italian custom boots; from the Rolex watch on his wrist to his diamond studded cuff links.

She guessed no one had told him it was dangerous to wear such expensive jewelry to this area. She'd met his type—they didn't last three days at the clinic before never coming back.

And Dana had heard enough about him to know that volunteering was something she'd never expected Josh to do. What was he doing here?

"Hello, Dana."

"Hi, Josh. What a surprise to see you here. I didn't take you for the charitable kind." Where had that come from? Why was she being snarky, unlike herself?

Josh leaned forward, his eyes locking into hers. "There's a lot you don't know about me," he responded in a low voice.

Want to read more? You can grab LOVING THE

BILLIONAIRE OWNER DOC at
https://dobidaniels.com!

Or want to know what happens next in
Dexington?
Sign up now at https://dobidaniels.com.

If you've loved reading Loving the Billionaire
Heir Doc, Dobi would be grateful if you could
spend a few minutes to leave a review (as short
as you like) on the book's page on your favorite
retailer. Your review would help bring it to the
attention of other readers. Thank you very
much.

Check out all Dobi Daniels books at
https://dobidaniels.com

ACKNOWLEDGMENTS

Writing a book is harder and more rewarding than I could have ever imagined. And it would not have been possible without the support, love, and encouragement from my number one cheerleader, my dearest mom. My life would never have been this awesome and wonderful without you.

Of course, I have to thank my precious little DC for his smiles and antics. You brighten my day and give me the strength to keep pushing through.

Thank you to my sisters for encouraging me on this wonderful journey. And a special thanks to my baby brother (who is so not a baby anymore) for being super supportive and checking in on my progress. You guys are the best.

Thank you to my wonderful author friends. You know who you are. Your selflessness and willingness to share what you know has made my writing journey smoother and an exciting one. And a special thanks to Lisa and Deanna whose support have made a difference.

Most of all, I want to thank God who gave me life, surrounded me with the most wonderful people, and loved me all the way. You make my life complete.

And finally, a special thanks to all my readers whose love of my stories spur me on to write more. Thank you!

As a former physician and business executive in another life—with a childhood filled with reading multi-genre novels—Dobi Daniels loves to write sweet thrilling romance stories with heart. She enjoys dreaming up everyday characters who rise above unfavorable circumstances to overcome incredible odds and find joy along the way.

When not writing, Dobi can be found binging K-dramas and ice cream with her little sidekick by her side.

Loving the Billionaire Heir Doc is the first book in the Dexington Doctor Billionaires Series. Sign up at dobidaniels.com to be notified when the next Dobi Daniels book comes out!

Thank you!

https://dobidaniels.com
hello@dobidaniels.com
facebook.com/dobidaniels
bookbub.com/profile/dobi-daniels
instagram.com/dobidaniels